MURDER

on the

33RD
FLOOR

A Corporate Mystery

*To Tammy,
With much
love and appreciation!
Mom*

B. KIM BARNES

For my co-author, Bev Scott, and all the internal consultants who contributed to our book, *Consulting on the Inside* (ASTD Press, 2011), with my affection and appreciation.

This book is a work of fiction, a product of the author's imagination. Any resemblance to actual events or persons, living or dead, is coincidental.

A Johari Press publication

Cover photograph by B. Kim Barnes

ADVANCE PRAISE FOR *MURDER ON THE 33RD FLOOR*

"Even though I've published 58 nonfiction books, I've been hooked on mysteries my entire life. Kim Barnes writes a well-paced whodunit that will keep you guessing and turning the pages. Kim's experience adds validity and her enthusiasm adds fun. This is a recipe for success. Get in line for Kim's next book; this is sure to be a successful series."

Elaine Biech
Author, *The Business of Consulting*

"I've never read a book about an OD consultant before and it was quite amusing to find myself being 'biographied' in the book - absent the murders, of course! Sarah's musings about concepts, tools, techniques, and methodology reminded me of my daily thoughts and the questions that surface as I do my work. It was like the words were coming out of my mouth! Her comment about 'why use the external consultant when I'm here?' was something I think. And some of her comments about people, fashion, and age were things I've actually said or thought, especially how to explain the job to others! I found myself paying as much attention to her OD comments as I did the murders. It was fun and think it would make a fun movie and educate people about OD!"

Lynne Andia
Senior internal consultant, global manufacturing firm

"Murder on the 33rd Floor is a fun read! It's not easy to describe what an OD consultant does but Kim Barnes has captured the profession perfectly in Sarah. She manages to delicately probe the corporate intrigue while maintaining her *professional ethics. While most of us have never had to deal with a murder investigation inside a company, thank goodness, we regularly wrestle with the corporate personalities and politics. Bravo!"*

Charlene Rothkopf
Executive coach, OD consultant, and former corporate HR executive.

"Move over, Dorothy Sayers! This book is the perfect complement to 'Murder Must Advertise,' as it gives the reader great insights on how an organization operates, and what is OD...This is 'OD for Dummies' on steroids!"

Veronique Rostas
Former internal consultant; executive coach and OD consultant

"A new detective mindset! B. Kim Barnes has given her readers a new approach to solving mysteries. Our smart heroine uses organization development tools – mind mapping, flip charts, and sticky notes – to solve a murder. Sarah's detective work is thrilling at the same time as she reveals the inner workings of her path to discovery."

Kris Schaeffer
Organization development consultant and avid mystery fan

"Barnes has woven a three dimensional story where her protagonist, Sarah, an internal organizational development consultant, reveals the tools of her trade while competently navigating ethical dilemmas and unraveling the '...layers of meaning and association that were unspoken...' at Martech, Inc. The third dimension of this fast-paced mystery is a treasure trove of information on special Bay Area places – making this book a must read for San Francisco residents and visitors alike."

Judith Olney
Former internal consultant and principal at Milestones LLC

"I just finished reading 'Murder On The 33rd Floor: A Corporate Mystery.' It is a very fun read – a romp through a mystery set in San Francisco. If you live in or know San Francisco, you will recognize the cultural and geographic references. If you do not know San Francisco, you will be introduced to its landmarks and personality. If you do business in the Bay Area, you will

chuckle at the familiar characters, settings and subplots. If you do not do business in the Bay Area, you may wonder how anything gets done here! If you are an organization development (OD) consultant, you will be tickled by the dynamics the heroine Sarah encounters. If you are not an OD consultant, you will see the world through the eyes of this fascinating profession. It is obvious that author Kim Barnes enjoyed writing this book. If you want a few hours of fun in a 'whodunit' novel, this little gem is for you."

Pat Newmann
Executive coach and consultant and principal at Ecstasis, LLC

"What an amazingly "novel" way to learn! Kim has always been uber-creative…and is at her best in this wonderful creation. Her deep knowledge of the field of organizational development come through loud and clear, as well as her decades of work in the field and her wonderfully warm and real writing style. This is a must-read for anyone in the field, or anyone who just plain wants a good read! The story goes quickly, you will truly 'get' the characters! It held my attention from beginning to end! Bravo to the author."

Beverly Kaye
Founder/Co-CEO, Career Systems; author, *Love 'Em or Leave 'Em*

"Kim Barnes' book Murder on the 33 Floor turns around the old cliché that consultants 'know where all the bodies are buried.' In her entertaining book, the bodies are real and the hero Sarah Hawthorne uses the skills of an OD consultant to find the killer. The book provides clever uses of OD terms and methods as Sarah investigates the mystery of what's happening at her company. OD consultancy meets Phillip Marlowe (or Jessica Fletcher) in a fun, quick read book that's a real page-turner. For the San Francisco reader, the Bay Area setting is enjoyable and adds a " Tales of the City" aspect to the book- and if you aren't an OD consultant, you will gain knowledge and maybe some new respect for what OD consultants do."

Charles Evans
Internal consultant, health care company

"Great murder mystery! Kim's writing style draws you in and keeps your interest from start to finish. I couldn't put the book down in anticipation of how the story would unfold. In addition, I loved how Kim brought San Fran-

cisco to life. Her accurate and colorful descriptions made me feel as though I was right there in the heart of 'The City.'

All of Kim's characters came to life and I particularly loved the realistic description of the main character and her profession of organization development. The steps she followed, thoughts she had, and actions she took were a fabulous portrayal of a person in this field."

Dena House
Director, Organization Development, high-tech company

PROLOGUE

"OD—where the rubber meets the sky." That was how Sarah Hawthorne's labor lawyer father used to dismiss her profession. She smiled. Only he could make that statement sound like a compliment…still, she didn't think he would say that now.

Sarah tapped her fingers on the steering wheel as she waited for the light to change. Takeout and a nice bottle of wine were all she had energy for tonight. She definitely didn't want to think about any more passive-aggressive clients. Early in her career, organization development (she preferred to use the official name of her field to fend off jokes about drug overdoses) was focused on issues such as quality of work life, team building, and helping managers deal with resistance to change. At least, that was true for people like herself, who were "internal consultants" employed by large companies. External organizational consultants were usually the ones called upon to guide leaders as they planned for and implemented major changes.

In recent years, though, some internal OD consultants, including Sarah, had graduated to the role of "business partner" to senior leaders—coaching and counseling them, providing advice during strategy sessions, and facilitating important meetings. Sarah had worked hard to earn the trust of the people at or near the top of her organization. She loved her job, but sometimes it was exhausting. One of her mentors, Peter Vaill, used to describe OD as "permanent whitewater." Having done some canoeing and rafting twenty years earlier, Sarah thought the description had only become more apt. She pulled into her driveway and pushed the "off" button of her hybrid car.

Sarah couldn't get the current drama out of her mind. For many weeks, Martech's merger with an innovative young company had dominated her life. Sarah frowned as she gathered up her bag and briefcase and stepped out of the car. "Merger" was the official word, but she thought it was more of an acquisition. Today's meeting had dealt with the conflicting demands of some key players. In her role as facilitator, she always tried to stay out of the content of the meeting while staying alert to subtle issues. In this case, though, she wanted to provoke the participants to deal openly with the conflict. It didn't feel like company politics as usual. Still, she intended to let it all go until the next day. Sarah was trying particularly hard at the moment to keep work and home separate—she needed a little more balance in her life. She opened the front door and called out to her husband.

It was the second week of January.

CHAPTER 1

January 13

Sarah's phone was ringing. It wasn't *When the Saints Go Marching In*, the sound she used for her wake-up alarm.

She swam up from a dream and picked the phone up from her night table just as it stopped ringing. She rubbed her eyes, squinted, and saw the number of the missed call; it was from her client, Ed. Why would he call her at, what, 3:00 a.m.? She waited a minute to see if a message icon would appear. Nothing. Dev, a talented sleeper, grumbled softly and turned over.

Sarah gave him an affectionate pat, got up quietly, and went to the kitchen; she was wide awake now. She turned on the electric kettle and pressed the "Call Back" button. The phone rang and rang. Odd. Maybe he had called her number by mistake? That would be unusual for Ed; he rarely did anything without a clear purpose. Of all her clients, he was the most self-confident leader. He rarely even solicited her help, other than to ask her to listen while he talked through a problem and a solution. She knew he valued her opinion, though he rarely asked for it directly. That made this call out of character, if it wasn't a mistake.

Sarah hesitated between herbal tea and her stash of strong black "selected leaf" Ceylon from Harrod's, a souvenir of a recent trip to England. There would be no more sleep, she decided. Caffeine it would be. Sarah poured the boiled water over the tea and set her mug down on the table. She took a sip too soon and burned her mouth. As she stirred the tea to cool it, she tried to reconstruct that meeting yesterday with Ed. Sarah often felt uncomfortable that her clients perceived her as a good listener and trusted advisor, and yet she rarely remembered details of the intense discussions they had had unless she had made notes. Fortunately, she was a quick thinker and had once been a promising jazz clarinetist. She could still "vamp 'til ready" when asked to pick up the thread of an earlier conversation. Sarah sighed and looked at the threads of morning fog that were now visible, swirling outside the window. She was, she sometimes thought, the perfect organizational consultant, as she was able to be deeply engaged when needed and then fade into the background. It was almost as if she existed for her clients only in those meetings, later diffusing like a fog might. She doubted that any of them thought of her as having a private life. She sometimes felt a little ambivalent about being the invisible woman.

Yesterday's events clicked into place in Sarah's mind as the caffeine kicked in. She and Ed had discussed an off-site meeting; what were the issues? Oh, yes. The merger was not going well. There was some conflict going on between two senior members of his team, and he wanted her to facilitate a problem-solving session. She had put it in her calendar with a note to interview the two managers next week.

Maybe ten years as an internal consultant in one company was too long. She ought to consider moving on; things were becoming too predictable. The merger would shake things up for a while, but she was in danger of becoming blasé. Organization development had seemed like an exciting career when she started graduate school fifteen years earlier. She had always liked walking the fine line between being an insider and an outsider. That was the story of her life, really. Never quite one thing or another—or, more precisely, something different to everyone who knew her. To Dev, she was a sturdy traveling companion, a competent bridge partner, an outdoorswoman with a soft spot for lost and bedraggled animals. To her grown daughter, a graduate of Harvard Law School and a practicing attorney, she was a somewhat scatterbrained but amusing ex-hippie. To her best friend, Alison, she was a sympathetic ear or intellectual sparring partner, depending on the day. To "newbies" in her field, she was a role model, a competent professional with an enviable seat at the table of senior executives. To her boss, Sylvia, head of Human Resources, she was a pleasant oddball with slightly occult powers for dealing with tricky situations and difficult people—someone who should generally be left alone. This suited Sarah very well.

One thing she definitely was not, as a rule, was introspective. Being up early and sitting by herself, reflecting, was not a regular part of her day. *Damn you, Ed*, she thought. *Before long, I will be pondering the meaning of life.*

She heard the newspaper hit the sidewalk, so she opened the door and went out into the fresh, cold, foggy air to retrieve it. Being up early had its compensations. She would read the op/ed columns on paper instead of virtually and do the crossword puzzle. In ink. She was proud of her ability to do that, although she pretended not to be. And maybe she would manage to get to the gym. Sarah was uncomfortably aware that the pound-a-year gain that her mother had correctly predicted twenty years ago had parked itself around her hips. Sarah had always appreciated the good genes that had given her a fairly narrow waist and what Dev referred to as a "nice shape" above and below it. Her features were unexceptional: brown eyes, a straight nose, full lips, and the remnants of a freckled childhood on her forehead and cheeks. Her straight brown hair had just a hint of salt and pepper. She was considering whether to color it, as Alison was encouraging her to do. Of course, Alison's colorist, like Alison, was a little more fashion-forward than Sarah. Well, actually a lot more.

Dev, a software consultant, worked from home. "You look remarkably awake," he said as she entered the bedroom to dress for work. Dev was tying his old blue robe over the pajama bottoms he often wore to work in on days that he didn't go to the gym. He was lean and muscular, just starting to fight the belly flab that even wiry men gain somewhere around fifty. He was blessed with hair that still needed thinning out when it was cut; the gray in it and his scruffy morning beard was just past "distinguished" and moving toward "iron."

"Give me a minute, and I'll get breakfast going." Dev's share of cooking chores ran to eggs in all forms and the occasional casserole.

"Don't worry about it. Why be an independent consultant if you can't sleep in?"

He threw a pillow at her. She caught it and grinned. "I've been up since three. I got a call from Ed, but he didn't answer when I tried to call back. He's never called me outside of work hours before."

"He was probably still at the office, thinking everyone should be on his schedule." Dev had a low opinion of corporate executives. His buddies were mostly professionals, consultants or entrepreneurs who worked their own hours and met one another at the gym or the local Peet's coffee shop.

Sarah reviewed her schedule as she drove to work. It would be a busy day with meetings, teleconferences, and a coaching session—typical for a Wednesday. She would probably need to go to bed early tonight, given the early start to her morning. *Thanks for that, Ed.*

Walking into her "corner office," a cubicle about the size of her bedroom closet, she noticed her message light flashing. Not everyone had her mobile number; she gave it only to friends and important clients. She found it odd that some colleagues put their cell number on their business cards. No personal life, she supposed. Only at work did she leave behind Sarah the person—wife, mother, friend, musician, hiker, animal lover. Here, she was Sarah the consultant. For some reason, the message light seemed particularly urgent this morning. She dropped her briefcase and bag, pulled out her faux Aeron chair, slid into it, and typed in her code.

CHAPTER 2

January 13

The voice on the recording had an odd edge to it. It was Ed's executive assistant. Nobody was called a secretary anymore, but that's what Penny was, and a good one too.

"Sarah, Penny here. Have you heard anything from Ed? He wasn't in when I got here this morning. He's got an early meeting to prepare for. It's not like him to be late, and he doesn't answer his cell. I'm checking with you, because there's a note on his desk that says, 'Call Sarah' with two exclamation points."

She picked up the handset and dialed. Penny answered on the first ring. "Hello, Penny. In fact, Ed did call me," Sarah said. "At 3:00 a.m. I thought it must have been a mistake, as he didn't leave a message. No answer when I tried him."

"I'm worried," Penny said after a brief silence. "This is really unusual. I tried his home number, but there was no answer there, either. Of course, he lives alone since his divorce." Sarah had not been aware of the divorce. Her relationship with Ed had been entirely professional. "Would you mind coming up for a few minutes?" Penny went on. "I'd like to speak in person." Penny was not a person who asked for help easily, and Sarah thought she had better respond right away.

"Of course." Sarah crossed meeting preparation off her mental list. She pushed back from her desk and hurried to the elevator.

Martech, Inc., was a high-tech company, but it was old-fashioned in a lot of ways. Instead of a campus sprawled across a former almond grove in the Silicon Valley, the headquarters was primarily located on the top several floors of a modern high-rise building in San Francisco. The building reflected Martech's culture, sleek and sophisticated, on the surface, but hierarchical. Manufacturing was done offshore, so the building was all offices, cubicles, and conference rooms. Near the entrance to the building on the ground floor there was also an employee cafeteria, an auditorium, and a rather showy coffee bar, which was open to the public.

Sarah pressed "33." The elevator rose smoothly and quietly. She took a deep breath and consciously relaxed her shoulders as she got off. She didn't visit this floor every day; most of her clients were a little lower in Martech's food chain. Whenever she did have business here, she had the odd sensation that she was shorter than usual. Perhaps the ceilings were actually higher on the thirty-third floor. All of the executive offices were located here, along with the executive conference room. This was where Important Things happened, though most of the real work of the organization took place on the floors below.

Penny's desk sat in front of Ed's office. There were fresh flowers in a silver-colored vase; otherwise, her desktop was bare and shining. Her computer sat a little to her right on its own table. Penny jumped up from behind her desk, greeted Sarah, and gestured toward the office door. She was a short, brisk, dark-haired woman in her mid-thirties. She wore a gray business suit, of good material but not cut especially well; a white silk blouse with covered buttons; and a small burgundy scarf at her neck. Her tiny earrings were gold hoops. Penny's hair, usually perfectly smooth, was slightly ruffled today, but her face revealed nothing; she wore her business-as-usual expression. "I usually don't enter Ed's office unless invited, but when I got here, I noticed the door was open and I just poked my head in to see if he needed anything for the meeting. It was odd that he was not there, so I waited a few minutes, then went in to see if he had left me a message, but there was only the note about calling you."

Through the open door, Sarah could see the view out of Ed's office window behind his cluttered desk. The Bay Bridge, the East Bay in the distance, and the "Cupid's Arrow" sculpture along the

Embarcadero were visible. Sarah had often found herself distracted by the view during meetings. It was probably just as well that she worked in a windowless cubicle; she would never get anything done with a view like that.

"What time is the meeting scheduled?" asked Sarah. "And who is it with?"

"At ten o'clock, with Jen and Arthur." Those were the two managers who were in conflict. Sarah was just as happy she wasn't expected to sit in on this one. It was now just after nine. "Have you checked with them to see if he changed the meeting time or place?"

"I did that first. They both said no. That's when I called you. I think you should talk to them. They are both pretty upset about the current situation, and if Ed can't meet with them, maybe you can help." Penny clasped her hands together, then quickly unclasped them and dropped them to her sides.

Sarah hesitated. Was this part of her responsibility? Maybe Ed had overslept. If he was calling people at three o'clock in the morning, that wouldn't be surprising. Maybe he had forgotten to tell Penny and the others about a change in plans. He could be on a plane heading for Asia because of some emergency in one of the plants. Or perhaps someone in his family had become ill, and he was rushing back to wherever he came from. But something was beginning to flutter in the pit of her stomach.

Sarah pulled out her smartphone and checked her schedule. Nothing that couldn't wait. "I just need to reschedule a few things, Penny. Please ask Jen and Arthur to meet me in the conference room separately, Jen at ten o'clock and Arthur at eleven. And call me at once if you hear from Ed."

CHAPTER 3

January 13

Sarah returned to the conference room at ten o'clock and stopped in front of the closed door to collect her thoughts. Jen would have already arrived; she was always on time. Sarah took a breath and opened the door with the hand that held her briefcase. She carried a cup of tea with the other hand. She did not expect the catering staff to have provided a full setup in the conference room today, so she had brewed a cup in the refreshment center downstairs. "Hi, Jen. It's good of you to make time for me. I know you were supposed to be meeting with Ed this morning."

Jen, tall, and slim, with Nordic coloring, wore a simple gray silk blouse and black skirt. Her earrings looked as if they were designed by Paloma Picasso. Silver, abstract shape, both feminine and strong. Sarah had a tendency to judge other women based on their jewelry. Jen had excellent taste, in her opinion. Nothing flashy, but clearly expensive.

Jen sat halfway up, smoothed her black designer skirt, and crossed her long legs. Sarah set her cup on the table. She was suddenly conscious of how short her own legs were as she adjusted the imposing conference room chair downward to accommodate them.

Jen smiled, but then her face grew serious. "It's so unlike him." Her voice had a slight Northern European lilt. German, maybe, but Sarah had never asked. "I can't believe he would forget or blow it off." Jen poured herself a cup of coffee from the carafe on the table. There was always coffee.

Jen would never have missed a meeting with her own team; they shared very close and mutually respectful relationships. Her people knew how lucky they were and made sure that they had the best numbers in the division, which made it harder for Jen's peers to make snide insinuations about how she had made it from being a sales rep to having a very responsible managerial role in only five years.

Sarah opened her laptop. "What was to be the topic of today's meeting?" Her voice was level and calm. She stopped, sipped her tea, inclined her head to match the tilt of Jen's, and waited for a response. Sarah had long ago learned the power of silence to encourage others to speak.

"Well, you know that Arthur and I have been pitching two different approaches to getting the merger back on track." She tightened her jaw, emphasizing her high cheekbones.

"Wasn't that the topic of the off-site meeting I was going to facilitate next week?"

Jen crossed her arms. "It was. But yesterday Ed called and said an urgent decision had to be made, and we should meet today to thrash it out."

Sarah raised her eyebrows. "Those were the words he used?"

"Yes. It sounded ominous. I wasn't looking forward to it." Jen shook her head and tucked a wayward strand of blond hair behind her ear.

"What did you think might happen?"

"I suspected Ed had decided to implement Arthur's 'Attila the Hun' approach."

Sarah looked up from her laptop. "How would you describe that?"

"Arthur recommended a wholesale firing of the Staticon leadership." Jen's accent became stronger. "My position is that we should find out what they have to offer us in the way of new ideas and talent before sending them away." Jen paused and shook her head. When she spoke again, her English was perfect. "Ed likes Arthur's tough approach. Everyone thinks he has tapped Arthur as his successor."

"What would that mean for you?"

Jen opened her mouth but didn't speak. Sarah waited in stillness a long moment. The motion detector in the conference room decided there was no one there and the lights went out. Jen frowned. Sarah waved her arm to alert the automatic meter and the lights flickered back on.

Jen took a deep breath. "That would certainly spell the end of my career at Martech. I could never work for Arthur." Her voice wavered a little as she spoke.

"That would be tough on your team." Sarah sat back a little.

"I think they lean on me too much now, but they are quite capable of operating on their own."

Sarah paused; her hands poised above her laptop, and considered how to frame her next question. "Are you convinced that you have lost the battle to Arthur?"

"I still hope I can influence Ed to consider my approach. I've put a lot of my energy into this company. I don't give up easily." Jen brushed an imaginary crumb off her skirt; then stood up to leave. "But I am exploring some options. There will be a time to exit stage left, perhaps soon." The theater metaphor resonated with Sarah for a moment. Perhaps the slight accent she noticed was the enunciation of a trained actress?

Sarah rose to her feet and offered her hand. "Thanks, Jen. I will get back to you if I hear anything."

"I appreciate your making time to see me this morning, Sarah." Jen stood and walked out with the confident stride of a runway model, steady on her stilettos.

Sarah reviewed her notes; then compared them with notes she had made in her meeting with Ed yesterday. *It seems odd*, she thought, *that Ed never mentioned to me that he was nearing a decision on how to move the merger forward. Wasn't that an open question to be discussed at the meeting she had been planning to facilitate for him? Clients, even the best of them, didn't always tell you what you most needed to know in order to be helpful to them.*

Arthur was due in ten minutes. Sarah had her doubts about him; he had always seemed a little too smooth to her. He had only been with the company for a year, but his résumé was impressive, and he was seen as a "water-walker" by some of the senior leaders. He was known to be good at "managing up," but many of his team members were unhappy. Some of the better ones had already left for other jobs and had spoken to Sarah on their way out, so she was aware of his management style. *If you can call bullying and playing favorites a management style*, Sarah thought.

"Hello, Arthur." He was a man of medium build with just the hint of a belly—Sarah suspected him of being a customer of "shapewear" for men—and a hairdo that was perilously close to a comb-over. She caught herself and slipped back into her nonjudgmental persona.

Arthur had a smooth, practiced handshake. "Sarah, it is good to see you." He dropped into one of the chairs, opened a bag, and pulled out a huge, sugarcoated muffin. "I'm very concerned about Ed. He is usually a model of reliability. It's one of the reasons I was willing to go to work for him. I had a number of other attractive options, as you know."

Sarah barely kept herself from rolling her eyes. "What was the agenda for the meeting this morning?"

Arthur studied the ceiling somewhere over Sarah's left shoulder. "We were going to finalize plans for refocusing the acquisition." Arthur's phone rang; he used the teeth-rattling ringtone that sounded like an old dial telephone. He answered it. "Of course you should have asked me about it! Did you think I wouldn't find out? Don't give me an apology, make it right!" With his lip curled, he clicked off, then winked at Sarah. "This generation is useless when it comes to doing real work. They need a strong hand at the helm."

This performance was consistent with what Sarah had been hearing from both current and former members of his team. He was a "screamer"; he didn't hesitate to humiliate people publicly for the slightest mistake; even for situations that were outside their control. In addition to the ones who had left already, at least two of his most talented team members were actively seeking other jobs. Arthur was no more popular with his peers; they avoided working with him whenever possible. They knew that Arthur would take credit for any success and blame them for any failures. Sarah had often wondered why Ed seemed to be unaware of the problems Arthur caused. Or perhaps he didn't care?

"Tell me a little more about the plans." Sarah was good at drawing out pertinent information and putting it together later, like a puzzle. Dev called this process her "inner detective."

Arthur settled back in his chair and put his arms behind his head, taking up as much space as possible. "I've been telling Ed that we should just cut our losses and avoid a lot of trouble by providing severance packages to the Staticon guys. We have plenty of good people here, and without the complication of aligning our approach, we could respond to the market more quickly. I think Jen has had Ed's ear; you know how he likes to spend time with her." Something close to a leer crossed Arthur's face. "And who wouldn't, of course. But she is too soft to be a good businesswoman. I think he was finally starting to see it my way. I assumed he would announce that at this meeting, and we could get on with making the changes and getting back to business. All this stuff about merging cultures is just so much woo-woo as far as I'm concerned." He grinned and winked at Sarah. "Oh, sorry, I forgot you make your living on woo-woo. Just joking."

Sarah bit her lip, took a long breath, and refused the bait. "Do you have any clue about where he might be today, Arthur?"

"No, and frankly, I am quite put off by being treated in this way. I know you will not share this comment with him, but it is rather cavalier to ask me to clear my calendar for the morning and then just not show up." Arthur smoothed the hair over his bald spot and tipped his chair upright again.

Sarah made a noncommittal sound and then suggested that he call her if he heard anything from Ed later today. Arthur agreed and walked out of the room, leaving his chair at a rakish angle and his empty bag and muffin crumbs on the walnut tabletop.

CHAPTER 4

January 13

It was a very strange day." Sarah settled down on the sofa after dropping her bag on the entry table. Dev opened a bottle of the Italian Sangiovese that he had bought a case of last week—an act that had led to an hour's friendly argument about supporting local industry. California was running out of everything except wine, Sarah had said, "and at least we should buy something that comes from here." Right now, though, the Italian red looked appealing, and she was ready to relax. They saluted one another and drank.

"How did things go today?" Dev was much better about asking her about her day than she had been when their roles were reversed. At that time, she had resented what seemed to her like Dev's interesting work life: the people he saw, his projects, what looked to be his inevitable rise up the corporate ladder. Her life seemed exceptionally dull with childcare, volunteer work, and then the grind of graduate school. But then Dev's company merged with—well, was acquired by—a larger company, and he was out of a job. She finished her degree and, a little to her surprise, was quickly hired by a small but growing manufacturing company. Organizational consulting suited Sarah very well. She enjoyed the diverse projects and the chance to interact with people from all levels of the organization, helping them solve problems and implement changes. Five years later, a job had opened up at Martech. Alison worked there in marketing and had told her that there was an opening for an OD practitioner. Sarah thought she had flubbed the interview, but the hiring manager told her he liked her straightforward manner. Perhaps being a fellow jazz musician did not hurt; he played in a local band himself. Today, she felt almost as confused and uncomfortable as she had felt during her first week there. She had never before had a client simply do a bunk and leave his or her problems for her to deal with.

Over a dinner of leftovers from last night's restaurant meal, Sarah said, "I spent two hours with the people Ed was supposed to see today. I got a sense of the way the meeting might have gone, if it had taken place. But Ed never showed, never called. I feel as if I should do something, but what? I'm not his manager, not a family member or close friend. Maybe he doesn't want to be found."

"What does your 'inner detective' think is going on?" Dev refilled their glasses and sat back.

"I'm not sure. I think he planned to be there, but something stopped him. It seems like he would have called otherwise. I tried his cell again at the end of the day, but I got the usual outgoing message, saying he'd call back in a few minutes. Of course, he didn't."

"How well do you know this guy? Is he the type to run off to Mexico or Morocco with a few mil that he embezzled? Or might he be an undercover spy for a competitor? An axe murderer?"

Sarah had to laugh. Ed was as straight an arrow as she had come across at Martech.

"He's been with the company for five years. I would think if he were after trade secrets, he would have found them some time ago." Sarah hesitated a moment. "And he's not a financial guy; he once confessed to me that he has trouble reading a balance sheet. I think he'd make a lousy embezzler." But Dev's half-joking query had planted a seed of doubt in Sarah's mind. How well did she really know Ed?

Sarah could not shake the feeling that she should take some action regarding Ed, but it was too late to do anything tonight. Tomorrow she would speak to Ed's boss, Roberta, the chief operating officer. If anybody knew anything relevant, it would be Roberta. Sarah left Dev watching a Mad Man rerun on his laptop and went to bed.

CHAPTER 5

January 14

"Is Ed back?" Sarah was pretty sure of the answer she would get from Penny but wanted to be certain before calling Roberta's office. She was right. Penny had had no word of or from Ed since yesterday.

Roberta's schedule was tight, Sarah persuaded Roberta's executive assistant to squeeze her in late in the morning. *She must know that Ed has disappeared by now*, thought Sarah. Sarah had never worked directly as a consultant to Roberta. At the highest level, the execs worked with external "guru" coaches and business advisors. Sarah had, however, facilitated a number of meetings for Roberta's team, and the two of them had a cordial and mutually respectful relationship.

Just before eleven o'clock, Sarah stepped off the elevator on the thirty-third floor and headed for Roberta's corner office. Tom, Roberta's executive assistant, greeted her. He was an impeccably dressed young man with an engaging grin and a slightly affected manner of speaking. When Tom was first hired, he was sometimes referred to (especially by the more senior administrative staff) as Roberta's "eye candy," but his friendliness and willingness to help others soon won over even his most skeptical detractors.

"Sarah, so good to see you," intoned Tom. "We are all *mystified* by Ed's absence. You are the closest we have to an in-house gumshoe. You must know *everything* that goes on here!"

"Tom, I'm lucky if I remember where I put my car keys. Keeping track of anyone else's whereabouts is not in my job description." Sarah smiled. It was hard to stay serious around him. He really was a bright light in an otherwise staid environment. Even his tie—silk, finely made, but in a screaming shade of lettuce green—was just barely within the bounds of the thirty-third-floor dress code, which was unstated but fiercely enforced by disapproving stares.

"I think Roberta is ready for you now." Tom ushered her to the door, knocked formally, then stepped back as Roberta called her in.

Like Roberta herself, the office was understated, clearly expensive, but in the best possible taste. Roberta rose from her seat behind a polished table. A gray and mauve sofa and chairs were placed so that visitors could enjoy the view of the Bay, sparkling on this sunny winter day. There were paintings on the wall by recognizable Bay area artists; the quiet interior scene with a man and a woman seated across a table must be by Elmer Bischoff. Sarah regretted her own lack of artistic ability but tried to make up for it through appreciation of the work of others. She especially liked the figurative paintings informed by abstract expressionism that were popular around the middle of the twentieth century in San Francisco. Roberta's taste was much like her own. For a moment, Sarah envied her this beautiful setting. Then again, she probably would not have cared for the responsibilities that went along with it.

Roberta, a slim woman, probably in her late forties, wore a simple black suit and pearls; her prematurely silver hair was cut in a short, elegant style. She greeted Sarah with a strong handshake and a worried expression. "I hope you have news of Ed. Penny told Tom that he called you."

Sarah gravitated to one of the chairs, noticing that it was at a comfortable height. She often felt out of place in the other executive offices, where most of the chairs seem to have been designed for people who were at least six feet tall. Sarah's long torso made it easy for her to be eye-to-eye with people when sitting, but when her feet did not reach the floor, she felt rather ungrounded, like a child in a grown-up's place. She appreciated the subtlety of Roberta's design sensibility. "I am just as puzzled as you are," Sarah began. "He did call me at three o'clock on Wednesday morning, but we never connected, and he left no message. It seems that nobody has seen or heard from him since then. Do you have any idea about what he was working on when you last saw him? Might something to do with a project have called him away?"

"I haven't seen him since I left for a meeting on Tuesday afternoon. I stopped by his office around three to ask him a question, but he wasn't there. As far as I'm aware, he's been completely focused on the merger. As you know, the Staticon culture is very different from ours; their systems are less sophisticated, and they're used to working in a much more 'ad hoc' manner. It hasn't been an easy meld. Still, they bring some really innovative technology and a number of big customers, so it's important to make it work. Of course, the merger is a huge financial investment for the company." Roberta leaned back in her chair.

"What is Ed's charter, exactly?" Sarah thought she knew, but it seemed important to check her understanding.

"He was basically the change leader, responsible for aligning the systems and integrating the key people. We don't want to lose everything that made us want to acquire them in the first place." Sarah sat up a little straighter. Had Roberta just referred to Ed in the past tense? She decided to probe a little deeper. In her role as an internal consultant, people told her things that they might not want to be generally known. Still, she seldom asked for information that was normally unavailable to people at her level. Internal consultants have to walk a very fine line to maintain trust with clients who may be three or four levels above them in the organizational hierarchy.

"How well was it going, in your opinion, Roberta?" Roberta's forehead creased for a moment. Sarah, adept at reading facial expressions, thought Roberta was deciding whether or not she ought to be open. Her pearls—understated, conventional, costly—revealed little about Roberta's personality and suggested to Sarah that she was very cautious about her image and about sharing information.

After a long pause, Roberta said, "Not well. Not well at all. I think we are in danger of losing some key talent, and some of their major accounts could walk away with them." Sarah let the silence go on for a while. She knew that Ed was one of Roberta's key subordinates; he had been entrusted with a very high-profile project. If it did not go well, it would reflect badly on Roberta. She leaned forward slightly.

"Ed was not as effective a change manager as I had expected him to be." Roberta took a deep breath and let it out slowly. "His attitude often came across to the Staticon people as arrogant—'my way or the highway.' More than one of their senior executives has complained to me. They had the impression that he was looking for a way to get them to leave."

Sarah uncrossed her legs and sat up a little straighter. She did not want to seem invasive, but she sensed from Roberta's tone of voice that there was something more there. She leaned forward slightly. "What actions have you considered?"

"Well, frankly, I have been seriously thinking about giving Ed his walking papers." Roberta touched the short strand of pearls around her neck, and her mouth snapped shut. She briskly stood up and gestured toward the door. "Thanks for the chat, Sarah. I have another meeting starting in five minutes. I know I can trust you to keep what I have said confidential. Let me know if you hear anything."

CHAPTER 6

January 14

Sarah dodged out of the rain and into her favorite bar in North Beach. It had been under the same management for forty years and looked it. The floors were clean, but scuffed. There were framed photos of long-dead film and sports celebrities on the walls, signed with warm wishes to the owner, of whom there were several badly painted but loving portraits here and there. Postcards from patrons wearing t-shirts with the bar's logo and standing in front of various tourist sites were prominently displayed near the bar, along with flags from the various contrades of Siena; the neighborhoods that competed in the Palio.

She scanned the room. All the scratched, but polished, café tables were taken, but then a couple stood up near the back. Sarah moved deliberately toward them so that she arrived just as the graying older man helped his companion, a much younger woman, into her coat. Sarah sank down as they left, happy to have a moment to relax before Alison arrived. They had met for a drink almost every Thursday for the past five years, ever since Alison quit working for Martech in favor of a senior position in a nearby public relations firm.

Even though it was a good career move for Alison, Sarah had insisted at first on these weekly meetings out of concern for her friend, who had just endured a very difficult divorce. Before long, though, Alison had plunged back into the single life, moving from Marin County into The City (there was never any confusion in the Bay Area as to which city you were referring to in that way). Since that beginning, "Girlfriend Thursday" had become a cherished tradition with them. Unless one or the other happened to be out of town, they never missed it.

Alison entered the bar, waved at Sarah, hung her coat on a rack, and stopped to order a mixed drink from the bartender. *Uh-oh, looks like man trouble*, Sarah thought, trying to remember what Alison had said last Thursday about the guy she was dating. What was his name? Oh yes, Ben. Sarah usually took public transportation to work on Thursdays in case the two glasses turned into three. Today might be one of those days.

Heads turned as Alison walked toward Sarah's table. She was dressed, as usual, in an outfit that would have looked ridiculous on Sarah or anyone less than six feet tall, but Alison carried it off with panache. Her longish skirt was a dark, rich shade of purple, ruched up in two places in the front. Her top was made of heavy black silk with a large portrait collar. It probably had wires inside it, as it seemed to stay where Alison put it, framing her expressive face almost like a Mary, Queen-of-Scots ruff. She wore earrings of colorful, semi-precious stones, which danced and sparkled as she moved.

Alison gave Sarah a one-armed hug, then sat down across the table, her earrings glittering in the low light of the bar. She set her drink down, sighed audibly, and settled into one of the old-fashioned café chairs. Alison's body, all six glorious feet of it, seemed too large for the chair.

A waiter lit the candle on the table with a cigarette lighter and took Sarah's order, a Sonoma Valley Zinfandel. After he left, Sarah said, "What's new? How are things with Ben? You were going to have 'the talk' this week, right?"

"Ben is history. I Googled him and discovered that he is still married. Why do these guys act as if we are too stupid to check them out?" Alison leaned her chair back against the flocked red wallpaper, a relic of the '60s. She let the front legs come back down with a thump. Alison's makeup was, as usual, perfectly applied, but her long hair—chestnut this month—was damp from the rain and clung to her forehead. She pushed it back and shook her head. "Men!"

Sarah bit her tongue and didn't point out that it had taken Alison six weeks to get around to vetting him.

A hint of regret passed across Alison's face. "He did have good taste in restaurants, though."

"I remember that he took you to Masa's and Gary Danko."

Alison giggled and rolled her eyes. "I think he put them on his expense account. Business dinners. Not sure his company knew what kind of business he was up to." She paused. "Nor did his wife, evidently."

Sarah leaned back and waited while the waiter delivered her wine. "At least you got some good meals out of it. The last guy used to take you to Freddie's Sandwich Shop."

"The starving-in-a-garret poet. Yes, but he did get the proprietor to name a sandwich after me, and he always ordered it. That was his idea of romantic."

"At least all of your boyfriends are bad for you in different ways. I would really worry if you kept making the same mistake!" Sarah raised her glass to Alison. "Here's to finding a single guy who's not poverty-stricken or a lying jerk like Ben. Oh, and straight." Sarah was remembering another recent liaison of Alison's with a golf pro, who, as it turned out, was just looking for a presentable woman to take to events.

"Yes, it took me a little while to appreciate that the 'peck at the door and nothing more' was not just old-fashioned gentlemanly behavior." This cracked both women up, and they had to put down their glasses to avoid spilling their drinks as they laughed.

After a pause to catch her breath, Alison asked, "What's going on for you, Sarah? How are things at work?" She drained her Cosmo, then put on her reading glasses and reached for the wine list. Sarah's fairly uneventful home life was seldom a topic for their table talk. Martech, however, almost always supplied interesting news or gossip, and on days like today, Sarah was grateful to have an outlet. While she never talked about her clients by name, Alison as well as Dev provided her with a way to test her thinking about a project or a person.

Today, of course, the topic of Sarah's conversation was Ed—or, rather, "a senior manager." "So in the end," Sarah summarized, "I don't know much more tonight than I did yesterday, and I feel as if I should do something, but I don't know what."

Alison put down the wine list and looked at her friend over her half-glasses. Her earrings caught the light, glittering as they swung back and forth. "Hasn't anybody called the police yet? Filed a missing persons report?"

Sarah's hands began to shake. She had to put her wineglass down. "It never occurred to me until this minute. Wouldn't that have to be his family? Come to think of it, I don't know whether he has any family, not close anyway. I just learned that he was divorced last year, and I've never heard him speak of children or siblings. Actually, his desk only has pictures of his boats. Not even a dog."

Alison called the waiter over and ordered a glass of Syrah. It arrived quickly; she saluted Sarah, still on her first glass. "If someone that senior goes missing for two days and never calls, texts, or e-mails anyone, I might assume that something is wrong. Not that I haven't wanted to disappear for a few days myself and leave my Blackberry at home."

"If you did that, how would you feel about having the police find you and drag you back?"

"You think he might be having a lost weekend in the middle of the week?" Alison's smooth brow furrowed.

"That doesn't seem likely—he's a pretty straight arrow. Or at least, that's what I thought until this happened." They moved on to other topics, but Sarah was uneasy. Sooner than usual, she finished her drink, stood up, and hugged Alison good-bye.

Sitting on Muni, San Francisco's light rail system, Sarah began going over worst-case scenarios. Ed was sick, he had fallen and broken a leg, he had been kidnapped by terrorists, he had fled to the Southern Hemisphere with ill-gotten gains, he had hooked up with a beautiful spy....Well, this was getting her nowhere. Why would he have called her in any of those situations? They were hardly intimate friends.

Dev had dinner waiting. She was the cook the rest of the week, but this was his contribution to Girlfriend Thursday. He repeated his two specialties on a rotating basis. This was a lasagna night. "Oh, by the way, honey, someone left a message for you on the answering machine."

"That's odd," Sarah said. "Everyone uses cell phones now. I don't even know why we keep the landline and machine. It's been ages since I've even checked to see if there's a message." She walked into the small room next to the kitchen. Originally a pantry, they had remodeled it and now used it as a home office. She listened to the message, frowned, then played it back again. It was from Roberta. She was speaking slowly. "Sarah, I'm sorry to call you at home. I don't have your mobile number. I need to talk with you the first thing in the morning. Please come and see me as soon as you get in. It's rather urgent." There was no callback number.

CHAPTER 7

January 15

Roberta's office door was open when Sarah got there. It was early; Tom hadn't arrived yet. Sarah knocked as a formality and stepped in, closing the heavy glass door behind her as Roberta requested. Roberta was impeccable in a white shantung suit and deep teal blouse. She wore diamond studs in her ears, Sarah noticed, rather than her usual pearls. Nothing at her neck. Her face was slightly flushed. "Please sit down, Sarah—oh, do you need coffee? Tom's just arriving. We may be a while."

"Black tea for me. Nothing in it." Sarah settled down on the comfortable chair. She would be grateful for some caffeine. Roberta buzzed for Tom and ordered their drinks.

"I found something strange last night," Roberta began abruptly. "I had deleted some sensitive e-mails about the merger on my computer, and I suddenly thought I had better make sure they were deleted on Ed's desktop. I do have his password as a precaution; we keep everyone's on file in case we need information in a hurry. Not very secure, I guess. By the time I got there, Penny had gone home. I half-expected Ed to be sitting in his office as if nothing was wrong. He wasn't, of course. But his shoes were. I saw them under his desk when I sat down to turn on his computer." Roberta wrinkled her brow. Her voice sounded a bit nasal, as if she had a bad cold. "Why would he leave his shoes behind? Maybe he went to the gym—but I've never seen him in workout clothes. I've always assumed he wears a tie to bed." Roberta sneezed and shifted in her chair.

"Did you check his computer?"

"No, the shoes spooked me. I suddenly thought that I had better touch nothing until...until..." Roberta's voice, usually cool and confident, trailed off. "I just walked out and closed the door."

"You sounded worried in your phone message. I assume you are considering taking some kind of action."

"I think if he doesn't show up or call today, we should call the police."

Sarah realized she had been holding her breath. And she noticed the "we." Whether she liked it or not, she was involved. "Maybe we shouldn't wait." As a consultant, she was used to helping others make decisions and remaining nonjudgmental. This time, she jumped at the opportunity to take action.

"This may seem odd," Roberta said, "but I'd prefer to call after hours. I don't want to alarm anyone unnecessarily." Her gaze dropped.

Sarah read between the lines. Roberta didn't want to excite the press. Things must be worse than she had thought with the merger, if press coverage was something to avoid. A concerned employer calling to report the disappearance of a valued employee—what could be wrong with having that appear in the news? And it was Friday, after all. Any unwelcome attention could blow over by Monday, replaced with the latest sports scandal or home invasion or financial meltdown.

Roberta moved her chair a little closer to Sarah. Her voice dropped. "Can you stay a little later today? I'd appreciate your support when I call. If I have to call." *Of course you'll have to call*, thought Sarah. She doubted that anything would change before five.

Walking back toward the elevator, Sarah wrestled with her conscience. She was used to supporting others in taking action rather than being a prime mover herself. She understood Roberta's hesitation, though she did not really approve of it. What if Ed was lying hurt or ill somewhere? A few hours could make a difference. Maybe she should make the call. That would mean pre-empting Roberta. Doing so would probably mean her job—but if it were the right thing to do, she could live with that. At least, Sarah thought, I can try to get her to change her mind. She turned back, only to see Roberta disappearing into her office with the CEO, Todd. There was no way she could get to Roberta now; Tom would never interrupt that meeting. She would call early in the afternoon.

Around two-thirty, Sarah had just finished the last of a series of interviews for a change project involving one of her clients, Mike, who managed a large IT group. His group was absorbing a number of people from Staticon, and they were about to institute some major process changes in the way they accepted and prioritized projects. It was the kind of project that Sarah could almost do in her sleep—people weren't so different from one another, after all. Some people saw the change as an advantage and were confident of their ability to master it. Others were suspicious that it was a set-up to replace them. Sarah could have identified the issues without interviewing anyone, but this way everyone was engaged and felt that their concerns were being taken into consideration. Which they were, Sarah knew. Mike was a good manager and a good human being; she always enjoyed working with him. Her dad would have called him a "mensch," one of those Yiddish words for which there is no exact English translation. Still, as part of the merger process, Mike would eventually have to decide who would stay and who would go; so the suspicions had some basis in fact.

As Sarah walked back to her office, she turned her cell phone on. She saw that she had a message from Roberta. She pressed the message button and began to listen, then stopped abruptly, put a hand on an empty desk to steady herself, and replayed the message from the beginning. In the first part, Roberta sounded hoarse, almost asthmatic, like she was having trouble breathing. What was she saying? Sarah could make out only a couple of words. Cabinet. Ed. Then she heard Roberta take a couple of shaky breaths. Her voice calmed as she explained what had happened. The cleaners had taken their opportunity to work on Ed's office in the early afternoon, as they noticed that he was not at his desk. Penny had agreed; she was on her way out for a doctor's appointment. They had found something terrible.

Roberta continued. "The police told me about it. The cleaners were dusting the heavy walnut cabinet in Ed's office and...

and they noticed a peculiar smell. If it was there yesterday, I wouldn't have noticed because of my cold. They thought it might be spoiled leftovers from a lunch at his desk...." There was a long pause. "When they opened the cabinet doors, Ed rolled out. In the fetal position; no shoes. Necktie pulled impossibly tightly around his neck." Another pause. "Please come as soon as you can."

Sarah froze for a moment. Her mind was racing. She could feel her pulse hammering in her chest. "Breathe, breathe." Slowly she composed herself and turned away from her desk, going over what Roberta had told her as she walked along the corridor of cubicles. She looked straight ahead, avoiding eye contact with her co-workers and trying not to appear flustered.

As she walked, Sarah focused on her understanding of the situation. She knew that the execs sometimes took Friday afternoons off to play golf or go to their weekend getaways, so the cleaners would take advantage of this to start earlier on the thirty-third floor. That way, they could have a more relaxed Friday themselves. Not today. The policemen were probably still in Roberta's office. Her call had come in only about fifteen minutes ago. Sarah quickened her pace toward the elevator.

As Sarah rushed by the conference room, she noticed a policewoman sitting with the two cleaners. The glass windows were designed, she supposed, to let the world know who was and wasn't included in important meetings. She couldn't hear the conversation, but the cleaners' gestures were animated, and the policewoman was making rapid notes on a tablet computer.

Roberta seemed to have regained her composure by the time Sarah arrived. There was a slight tic below her left eye, and her right foot was jittering beneath her carefully crossed ankles, but her voice sounded cool and professional. "Thanks for getting here so quickly, Sarah."

"Hello, Roberta." Sarah turned and introduced herself to the two policemen—one black, one Asian—who were sitting on the sofa. "Sarah Hawthorne. Organization development consultant."

"I'm Sergeant Harry Belmont, and this is Inspector John Chu."
The uniformed sergeant nodded toward his companion, who was
dressed in plain clothes.

"You knew the deceased well, Ms. Hawthorne?" Inspector Chu
spoke first.

"I knew him professionally. He was my client."

"You are a sort of therapist, then?" Sarah was used to people not
understanding her role. She had long since given up explaining it to
older members of her family. "No, I'm an organizational development
consultant. I help managers and executives in this company make
decisions and implement changes."

"Then you were aware of his absence the past two days?"

"Yes, I was informed about it. I had been working with him to
plan an off-site meeting." Sarah wanted a few answers herself. "How
did he die? When?"

"We don't have enough information as yet," the sergeant answered.
"We understand that you were the last person to speak with him."

"That's not quite right," Sarah said. She leaned forward. "He
called me at 3:00 a.m. on Wednesday, but I was asleep and missed
the call. When I called back, he did not answer."

"Is that a normal practice?" asked Inspector Chu. "You must have
been very close to him."

"Not at all," said Sarah, sitting up a little straighter. Was he suggesting that they were having an affair? She supposed that might leap
to a policeman's mind; she made an effort not to take it personally.
"That was totally out of character. It had never happened before. I
have no idea why he should have wanted to speak with me at that
hour." Why did she feel a little guilty? Did she think she might have
saved him if she had answered in time?

"But you did call him back, didn't you?" persisted the policeman.

"Yes, I guess I was curious. It was an odd thing for him to do. I try
to be responsive to my clients."

"We will want to speak with you at some length, Ms. Hawthorne."
Inspector Chu, who looked to be about ten years younger than Sarah,
looked directly at her and nodded sternly.

Sarah remained cool, with some effort. "I am at your disposal, gentlemen. I will be here all next week. Or will you need to speak to me over the weekend?"

"Just leave us a number where you can be reached in case we have some urgent questions."

"Of course." There was an odd buzz in Sarah's ears. The whole situation seemed unreal, like an episode from a television series she used to watch; she couldn't recall its name. Things like this didn't happen at Martech. They certainly didn't happen to her.

Sarah wished she could speak to Roberta, whose calm demeanor was unconvincing. Did she need support? And if so, how could she offer it? "Roberta, would you like a ride home?"

"Thanks, Sarah. I need to be here until these gentlemen are finished. And, someone is coming to move the...er, to take Ed's body away. I think I should stay. Someone needs to sign something, I think."

No family or friends. Nobody to sign anything except your boss. A bad end, thought Sarah.

CHAPTER 8

January 15–18

"The shoes," Sarah mused to Dev that evening. "Why would he have taken them off? Or why would someone remove his shoes after...I mean before putting him in the cabinet?"

Dev, who had just finished a major project and would have liked to enjoy a relaxing and perhaps romantic evening with Sarah, had a practical engineer's response to the question. "Ed was a big guy, right? He probably didn't fit in the cabinet with his shoes on."

Sarah smiled and then felt guilty about it. Ed had been her client and an important person in the company. And a human being. Now he was dead. For the first time since she had heard the news, she allowed herself to continue to the next logical thought. *Someone killed him. Someone I might know.*

Dev seemed to read her thoughts, as he often did—sometimes to her displeasure. Being married to someone for a long time had both benefits and drawbacks. She sometimes wished she traveled more often on business; she always appreciated Dev more when they had been apart for a while. They had a good marriage, and she was grateful for that; her first husband had been an alcoholic, a narcissist, and a social climber. Bad combination. Still, there were days when she would have liked a little more space.

"Maybe you have a theory about what happened. You probably know a lot more about what goes on in that company behind the scenes than anyone else."

"I do. Or at least, I thought I did. But I don't have a clue as to why anyone would want to kill Ed."

The weekend was busy. Sarah's daughter Astrid (Sarah's first husband was part Norwegian) had recently announced her engagement to another Harvard-trained lawyer in her firm. The two families met for an awkward but expensive dinner at Postrio. Sarah did her best to describe her work when asked. The parents made polite noises and quickly changed the subject to golf. The police did not call.

Driving to work on Monday morning, Sarah decided that Dev was right. She had been at Martech for a long time, and she often remarked to Alison that she knew where the bodies were buried. Not a very attractive phrase, she now realized, but perhaps truer than she had thought. Everything she had discussed in the past several days in relation to Ed had something to do with the merger. Maybe the merger was relevant to Ed's murder. She would need to think very hard about that.

In her career at Martech, Sarah usually managed, as she had been trained, to stay focused on process and professional issues rather than the content of what her clients were talking about. Unless asked to give her professional opinion about the "people aspects" of a business decision, she seldom recorded or retained much detail about the decision itself. That made her a trustworthy consultant; one can't spill the beans about something one doesn't really understand. She smiled briefly; her father would have appreciated her self-deprecation.

Sarah made a mental list of what she did know regarding the merger. To the annoyance of her internalized English teacher, she found that she was thinking in bullet points.

- Martech was twice the size of Staticon, both in revenue and employees.
- Staticon had several new products in development or production that were considerably superior to similar products in Martech's major line of business.

- Staticon was a private, family-owned business, whereas Martech was publicly traded. The family had decided to sell, it was rumored, because of the debt load and some potential legal issues with one product.
- The employees of Staticon were said to be very unhappy with the decision; some of the key players had believed that the family would offer an ownership stake to them eventually. They were hoping to be near the front of the line at an IPO (Initial Public Offering).
- The cultures of the two organizations were like night and day. Staticon was a typical Silicon Valley upstart. Other than being family-owned rather than venture-funded, it was like other high-tech firms, with a campus setting, flat organizational structure, flexible processes, and no dress code. It was innovation-friendly, slightly chaotic. It had even retained the traditional Friday beer bash—except soft drinks were provided after one round.
- Martech, on the other hand was high-rise, hierarchical, well organized, and structured, even bureaucratic. Martech generally bought its innovation by acquiring smaller companies. It was a formal culture. Polite. Alison called it "passive-aggressive" because of all of the "meetings after the meetings" where people said what they really thought. There was a great deal of political maneuvering behind the scenes.
- Not surprisingly, the merger was taking a long time to settle in, and there were a lot of problems with it. Conflict about how to merge all of the systems. Competition for decision-making authority. Open hostility between senior managers from each of the companies and a resulting split along "party lines" within supposedly merged groups. There were even complaints about the dress code, especially the part about having to wear closed shoes instead of sandals and (unheard of in Silicon Valley) no T-shirts.
- Ed's two senior direct reports were at odds about how to handle the situation. Jen took a more open approach, hoping to

bring people together to resolve the issues, and Arthur was in a "fire the bastards" mode. He had appeared to be winning Ed's support. Although Roberta, Ed's manager, seemed to favor Jen's approach, Arthur had a track record of bringing senior executives around to his position.

Sarah had viewed the merger as a coup for Martech, precisely because it had brought in new blood, people who could shake things up, perhaps reinvigorate the company. Still, as she thought about it, she could see that Martech's "organizational immune system" had been triggered. Staticon was clearly a foreign virus. It was not surprising that there had been so much kerfuffle in the past few weeks and months.

Entering the building, Sarah noticed that something was different. There were several people who were clearly not in on the Martech corporate dress code sitting in the coffee bar or standing near the elevators. She remembered how she and her college friends had prided themselves on being able to spot "the fuzz" working under cover at protest gatherings. *I haven't lost the touch*, she thought.

Security on the 11th floor was more thorough than the usual informal glance and greeting. Sarah turned on her phone as she walked into her office. She always left it off deliberately while driving, both to make sure she was not tempted to text or call and to provide a little space to think. There was a message on it from one of the policemen, Inspector Chu, the plain clothes guy. He would be in her office at ten to interview her. Sarah decided that her best approach was to say as little as possible while learning as much as she could.

CHAPTER 9

January 18

Inspector Chu arrived at the reception desk on the eleventh floor a few minutes early. Sarah was just finishing up some e-mails when she got the call from the receptionist. Her cubicle did not lend itself to private conversations, so she met the detective at the desk and then led the way to a small conference room on the Bay view side of the building where they could close the door.

"Call me John," the inspector said and smiled.

"I take it that you don't consider me a suspect, then." Sarah felt a little silly asking, but it seemed wise to check.

"Not at all, but I gather that you have sort of an 'inside baseball' view of the situation. I want to get some background that might shed light on why someone would want to kill Mr. Castleman."

Sarah shook her head. "I don't know if I can help. I have sort of a vague feeling of responsibility about this whole thing, as if I have a key or a clue to the truth—but if I do, I don't know what it is."

"Anything you can tell me about his recent work would be helpful. Who was involved, what were the issues or conflicts, that sort of thing." John's tone of voice was even; he crossed his long legs and settled back into the conference room chair.

"I've been trying to assemble the facts I know, mainly about the merger, as that is what he was working on. He and I discussed it many times over the past few months. I suppose that could be relevant." Sarah glanced at the notes she had made earlier and reviewed them with John without elaborating. As he listened to the points she outlined, he wrote in an old-fashioned spiral-bound notebook, then asked a few probing questions.

"You mentioned the two subordinates, Jen and Arthur. Were there any other key players in this merger drama?"

"I suppose you would have to include Bengt. He was the CEO of the acquired company. And his crew: Carla, the COO, Vijay, and Craig, his two senior VPs. They were the top team at Staticon, but I think they may be in the process of being forced out. With a golden parachute, of course."

"A what?" He looked puzzled. Sarah realized that she would need to avoid "corporatespeak" with Inspector Chu—er, John. He, no doubt, spoke "police," and they would need to communicate in their common language, plain English.

"A golden parachute is usually a large settlement of cash, stock, or other benefits offered to an executive you are asking to leave the organization. It has to be generous enough so they are willing to take the leap." Sarah smiled. She realized how often she used terms without thinking of their literal meaning. An odd picture formed in her mind of the Staticon execs lined up inside a small plane, being encouraged by Ed and others to jump.

"Do you think any of them harbored a grievance toward Mr. Castleman?"

Sarah reflected for a moment. This was not an exercise in strategic thinking or a planning interview. It was an all-too-real process of closing the net around someone she probably knew. Maybe someone she liked. She had to be careful not to cast suspicion on someone innocent—or to protect someone who might not be. Having a grievance was certainly not tantamount to having a motive for murder, she thought.

As for Bengt and his people, Sarah doubted that any of them was so desperate that they would kill Ed and stuff his shoeless body into a cabinet. They were the essence of cool, in a Valley sort of way, and surely had many options if this did not work out. "I never noticed anything that would suggest that," she finally responded.

"I'd like to ask a favor of you," John said. "I understand that you are trusted by these people. It would be very helpful if you would talk to the ones who were closest to the victim and see what you can learn. They are likely to be very closed-mouthed with me."

John's request shook Sarah. She took a deep breath to calm herself. While there was no Hippocratic oath for OD consultants, if there had been, this would certainly violate it. "I couldn't do that," she stated brusquely. "I always hold the contents of any interview as confidential; if I didn't, nobody would tell me anything."

"Sorry." John inclined his head slightly. "I understand you can't violate anyone's confidence. However, I would value any suggestions you have about who we should talk to. You don't even need to say why, and we would not divulge your role in the investigation. I'll give you a call later in the week. No pressure. And thanks." He stood up, offered his hand, and left the conference room.

Sarah's head was whirling. She hoped it was not the beginning of a migraine. She seldom got them now, but they had been frequent and crippling when she was younger. No visual disturbance, though, so maybe this was just stress. Had she just been asked to be a police informant? Her intention to say as little as possible had melted under John's friendly but persistent questioning. And she really hadn't learned much, if anything, from him.

Sarah seldom went out for lunch, but today she needed to get away from Martech to sort things out. She shrugged on her coat and headed for the small nearby Vietnamese restaurant where she and Dev had celebrated their last anniversary.

The fresh, crisp winter air felt good. Her head began to clear as she waited for the first traffic light to change. She walked the three blocks quickly, entered the small, uncrowded restaurant, and was seated immediately at a small table in the back. She studied the large menu, glad to be distracted for a moment. She wished she could read the posters on the wall, listing dishes she would probably like, if only she knew what they were.

Sarah glanced up, ready to give her order to the approaching waiter, then tried to duck back behind her menu as she noticed Arthur heading toward her table. It was too late. She would not have been glad to see him on an ordinary day, but she felt particularly unprepared to talk with him today. Arthur asked if he could join her at the same time that he was pulling out a chair and setting his briefcase down. Sarah would have liked to say no, but from someplace deep down, she called up a professional smile and a degree of what she hoped sounded like sincere pleasure at seeing him. Not that he would be able to tell the difference, Sarah thought, privately hoping for a moment that he would turn out to be the murderer. She immediately discarded that thought as unworthy of her.

"Quite a shocking situation, eh?" Arthur began. "I was telling my wife that I might have been one of the last people to see Ed alive."

Sarah arched her eyebrows. She was somewhat surprised to learn that Arthur was married. She had imagined, when she thought about him at all, that he spent lonely nights watching porn on his computer in one of the boring high-rise apartments that had been built over-looking the Embarcadero Freeway—but which now, thanks to the last big quake, had a view of the Bay. "When was that?" Sarah made herself engage in polite conversation. The waiter came by and took her order. Arthur had brought his own sandwich. He took it out of a bag and began to eat.

"Oh, he passed my office toward the end of the day. He was in a hurry and didn't have time to talk."

Sarah almost asked Arthur if Ed was wearing shoes but thought better of it. "How do you know he was in a hurry?"

Arthur lifted his chin a bit as if he felt offended in retrospect. "He didn't even look in, just responded to my greeting with a nod and kept on going. Walking very fast. I had something important to ask him, so I called after him, but he didn't answer. I waited for an hour or so, and then I had to leave. The wife was having company for dinner."

Sarah suppressed a shudder at his reference to "the wife" as if she were a piece of furniture. It occurred to her that Arthur would have fit quite well in a '50s ad agency. "What time did you leave, then?"

Arthur pulled back his left sleeve and performed an elaborate demonstration of looking at his watch; a knock-off, Sarah thought, of an expensive Swiss one. "It was six, so I suppose it was around five that I saw him."

"Have you told the police about this?" Her voice sharpened.

"Oh, yes. The police interviewed me right away. Said I had given them some very useful information." Arthur reached up and smoothed his sparse hair.

Arthur's self-importance was no doubt confirmed by the policeman's comment—as it seemed to be by most events. Solipsistic—that was the word that came to mind. Arthur did not actually believe anyone other than himself existed. He was clearly the center of the universe. She supposed he was glad to be able to talk to someone about his part in the drama. Perhaps he had followed her here for that express purpose. *If that's all there is to it*, she thought darkly. Her meal arrived. The food was not as good as she remembered, but then again, the companionship was not exactly enhancing the experience.

CHAPTER 10

January 19

Sarah paused as she loaded the Swedish dishwasher in the small but smartly appointed kitchen. The European appliances had been her idea. Dev thought this was a wasteful extravagance. The worst fight they had had during the remodel had been over the Wolf stove; according to Dev, it was a success as a status symbol, but otherwise impractical. Still, he had grown fond of using it, ironically to be sure, to bake one of his specialties, Martha's Company Casserole. This was a 1950s recipe he learned from his grandmother, involving hamburger and several kinds of cheese. It made his lasagna a diet dish by comparison.

Sarah closed the dishwasher, turned it on, and sat down. "Dev, I don't think this situation is covered by anything they taught us in graduate school. I'm not really sure what my responsibilities are in this investigation. Is it part of my job, or not? I don't think I actually have a client, other than the organization itself, maybe. I feel like I might know something that could help untangle the situation, but I don't know what it is, and almost anything I might say to the police would be bound to cast suspicion on someone who is completely innocent. I mean, I have certainly said things in anger that I wouldn't want repeated in a court of law."

Sarah straightened the place mats and picked up some dead petals that had fallen off the roses Dev had brought home early in the week. The dishwasher hummed quietly, almost tunefully, in the background.

"I guess you have someone in mind, then," Dev said matter-of-factly. He was an exceptionally good listener—*especially for an engineer*, Sarah always thought, and then would chide herself for stereotyping.

Sarah started to deny it and then realized he was right. She had been wondering if Jen had settled another matter with Ed—one she had been especially fired up about recently. Jen's request for approval to hire a young man from China had been pending for several weeks. He would require an H1B visa in order to get a work permit. They had been unable to find anyone local with this man's skills, skills that were needed to fill a real hole in the team. Ed was dragging his feet. Jen had confided to Sarah that she suspected that he was trying to prove a point linked to his political beliefs about immigration. She supposed that if the lack of this particular skill set caused her team to falter in completing their current project, he would not be sorry. Sarah had thought at the time that there must be a back story that she was not privy to. She had not, however, chosen to pursue the matter.

"Yes," she nodded at Dev. "I didn't even realize it until a moment ago, but there is someone I'm a little concerned about. I doubt that what she said to me has any bearing on the case. But I suppose they will be looking at anyone who had an axe to grind with Ed."

"You didn't make any promises to the detective, so maybe you can make some discreet inquiries. That way, you can satisfy yourself as to whether this or anything you turn up is relevant." Dev sounded, as always, like the most reasonable of men—which, in Sarah's estimation, he was. Most of the time, at least.

"In other words, just do what I usually do. And stay away from the police inquiry unless something seems relevant to their work, even if I think it is just normal corporate politics. That's when I would have to examine my values, I guess." Sarah rubbed her jaw a little, encouraging it to relax.

"Well," said Dev, "I would hope that if you stumble over any bodies, you won't have to check your old organization development textbooks for guidance."

He was only half-kidding, Sarah knew. He thought her insistence on following her profession's rigid code of values was just a little pretentious. They were almost like a mantra to Sarah: respect, inclusion, empowerment, authenticity, self-awareness, collaboration. Dev was more flexible. Short of stealing someone's property, whether tangible or intellectual, he didn't see that a professional code of values had much place in the business world. You just treated people the way you would want to be treated yourself, and when confronted with an issue, you trusted your instincts to point you in the right direction.

Sarah decided that she would try to see Jen in the morning. Dev's gentle prodding had helped free her to investigate the situation. It wasn't exactly in her job description, but she guessed there were some larger issues at work in the organization that she might come to comprehend better if she asked a few questions. And that, she justified to herself, was certainly part of her role.

Sarah had a restless night. She had the elevator dream again; her recurring dream for decades. She would get in and press the button for the highest floor. Others got on and off; then she was alone. The elevator rose rapidly and kept rising past the top floor. She would press the emergency button, but nothing happened. Just as it began to slow down, she woke herself up, as she always did. Maybe someday she would have the courage to see what was outside that door...but not yet.

CHAPTER 11

January 20

Jen was able to squeeze in a lunch meeting with Sarah; they walked over to the Ferry building to eat at the MarketBar. Jen was wearing a chic trouser suit in a light shade of green that enhanced her fair coloring. Sarah wouldn't have been able to walk half a block in Jen's shoes. She thought they might be Manolo Blahnik, but due to her serious lack of interest in high fashion, she couldn't be sure. Jen, however, moved as easily and gracefully as if she were strolling along a beach in her bare feet.

It was warm enough on this San Francisco winter day to sit outdoors, illustrating the inverse of the famous aphorism, "The coldest winter I ever spent was a summer in San Francisco," usually attributed to Mark Twain. There is some doubt that Mark Twain actually said it, but it is true that summer in San Francisco can feel like winter and vice-versa.

Sarah and Jen had been involved in a few projects together and had developed a great deal of mutual respect. Sarah's work, at its best, was almost invisible (she liked the Taoist saying that ended, "…as for the best leaders, the people say, 'we did it ourselves'"). Jen was one of the few people who observed and appreciated Sarah's subtle facilitation skills—drawing out a reluctant team member; summarizing long, complex discussions so that key issues became clear; encouraging alternate viewpoints and creative solutions to emerge from a previously unproductive discussion. She had once even expressed interest in the possibility of entering a graduate program in organization development and had asked Sarah's advice about which ones to explore.

Today, Sarah reminded herself, was not a regular social visit or professional meeting. She needed to set aside her own opinions and feelings about Jen and the others if she were to follow the path she had set for herself last night with Dev's support.

"Jen, how is your team taking the news about Ed?" Sarah began.

"They were shocked, of course—as was I. But..." Jen's brow was furrowed, and her shoulders hunched. She looked away from Sarah.

"But..." repeated Sarah, hoping to keep the words flowing.

"Well, some of my team members said some things that worried me."

"Such as...?" encouraged Sarah.

"Such as that they were surprised someone had not done it sooner." Jen stopped abruptly and studied the menu with great intensity.

Sarah recognized the signs—clients often felt that they had given Too Much Information to her. She proceeded very delicately. "I suppose they thought he had created some difficult issues in the company." The waiter arrived to take their order and told them about the daily specials. Everything sounded good, and the interruption was welcome, allowing Jen some time to think. The waiter wove his way through the tables back to the kitchen. Sarah continued, "You must have been shocked."

This empathetic response seemed to relax Jen; she sighed and sat back. "Yes, but I understood their feelings. The team has been doing their best to mesh the Martech and Staticon approaches, and they did not feel that Ed supported them, especially when he would not let us hire Lee—you know, the guy from Shanghai University that I was telling you about. They all liked Lee and felt that his skills were exactly what we needed. They now have to do some things they are not trained to do, and they resent it." Jen's usually melodic voice suddenly became harsh. Her level of bitterness seemed excessive to Sarah for the situation she had described. She probed deeper.

"What else do you suppose your team was upset with Ed about?"

"I'm not exactly sure. Perhaps they were feeling protective of me…there have been rumors about my future here…"

"I don't think I've heard them," Sarah said. She knew a lot about what went on in the organization, of course, but was often out of the loop of the informal gossip network, precisely because she tried to stay on the inside/outside edge, keeping enough distance to see the big picture; to be aware of the way the system worked.

"Oh, there has been talk of a larger restructuring when the Staticon merger process is completed. Someone from Arthur's team told one of my key guys that they expected Ed to merge our two groups—and force me out. Everyone is updating résumés in case that happens. Working for Arthur is not the most coveted opportunity among my team." Now there was acid in Jen's voice. Lunch arrived, and their talk turned to other topics.

"I really enjoy coming here. I know the ingredients come straight from the farmers' market and the fish and meat dealers inside." Sarah had been coming to the Saturday farmers' market at the Ferry Building ever since the landmark had been renovated and turned into a showplace for fresh food. "The Loma Prieta earthquake in '89 did a lot of damage; people were killed and buildings were destroyed, but it did make this area come alive because of the freeway collapse. After a lot of back-and-forth about what to do, they decided not to rebuild the freeway, but to widen the street instead, put in the old streetcars and the palm trees, and renovate the Ferry Building." Sarah assumed that Jen was not living in the Bay Area at that time and in any case would have been quite young when it happened. Jen nodded politely. Her face was turned to the sun, and her eyes closed for a moment. The waiter appeared with coffee and tea.

As they sat relaxing over their hot drinks, Jen said, "I'm glad you asked me to talk. I haven't slept well since last week. The police interview creeped me out."

Sarah was startled to hear Jen using slang. Her English was usually as sophisticated as her outfits. "How so?"

"They asked me the usual questions. You know, when did I last see Ed, what was my business relationship with him like, did I think he had any enemies. Then they all but suggested that he and I had been in a romantic relationship that ended badly. I suppose Arthur had put them up to that."

"And had you?" It was a much more direct question than Sarah had thought she would ask, but it escaped her lips before she could edit it.

"Well, yes. But it was a long time ago, not at this company. I had thought, hoped, rather, that the news had not reached Arthur, of all people. He is a classic backstabber."

"Why do you think it might have been Arthur who mentioned it to the investigators?"

"Well, I don't know for sure, but Arthur has often hinted that he knows something about my history that I wouldn't want to be made public. He used to come on to me, and at first I simply ignored it. Finally, I had to remind him of the sexual harassment guidelines from HR. Once he got the message, he began making unpleasant remarks to me whenever he could get away with it."

Sarah had envied Jen her looks from time to time, but she realized that being an upwardly mobile, beautiful blonde at Martech brought its own share of problems. "What did you tell the police?"

"They didn't come right out and ask me, just hinted. I didn't take the bait. But I suppose it may come up again if they decide I am a suspect."

Later, as Sarah was putting her laptop in her case, ready to leave for home, she turned the conversation over in her mind. She really had been taken aback by Jen's acknowledgement about her relationship with Ed. The rumor about them was one of the few she had heard (she didn't miss them all) but had dismissed as salacious gossip,

As she picked up her bag, the telephone on her desk rang. She considered not answering it, but set the bag down again. "Hello... Oh, Roberta, how are you doing? Yes, I could come up for a few minutes."

Sarah walked briskly toward the elevator lobby, curious about what Roberta had in mind. She might have decided to confide in

Sarah; perhaps she wanted to elaborate on what she had said the other day, or maybe she just needed to talk.

As it turned out, Roberta wanted something different. She spoke slowly and deliberately. "Sarah, you seem to have impressed the policeman in charge of the investigation with your knowledge and perspective. I would appreciate your taking on the role of liaison between the company and the police. I checked with your manager, Sylvia, and she approves of the idea. So does Todd. Someone needs to do it, and I think you have the right skill set. I don't think PR would be subtle enough." Sarah quickly got the meaning behind the word. "Subtle" would mean able to keep one's mouth shut.

This was a bit of a stretch. Roberta's boss, the CEO, sometimes known as "Todd, the Almighty," probably didn't even know who Sarah was. He prided himself on his ability to delegate and was not in the habit of "managing by walking around." In fact, that trend had come and gone many years before without affecting Martech in any way that Sarah could see, at least here on the thirty-third floor. She opened her mouth to say no, but the words that came out were, "Tell me what that would involve."

Roberta took that as agreement and said that she need do nothing more than meet with John Chu regularly until the matter was settled—and to keep the company's interests in mind as she did so. This didn't sound very different from what Sarah had already begun doing. "And check in with me from time to time to let me know what is happening. Oh, and one more thing. We continue to get inquiries from the press. PR has most of that covered, but there is one journalist who is trying to turn this into an exposé of corporate evil. If you don't mind, I'll have Tom refer him to you. His name is Seth something."

CHAPTER 12

January 21

Thursday was relatively calm, except for persistent calls from Seth. Sarah got deeply involved with a new project, a team startup with people from both sides of the merger. The two companies had very different assumptions about power, authority, and leadership. This inevitably led to a considerable amount of chaos and upset. "Forming, storming, norming, performing"—this was the mantra about group development that often ran through Sarah's mind as she thought about the teams she worked with. Bruce Tuckman had really hit on something back in the early days of OD (Sarah didn't often use that term out loud, because others immediately thought of drug emergencies. Baby Boomers did, anyhow.) During Forming, people tended to be polite and cautious. Once they were comfortable with their place in the team, they began to express opinions and disagreements, and conflict would ensue—that was Storming. Eventually, the group or team would agree on how they would operate and settle the major issues; Tuckman called that process Norming. And finally, the team was really ready to Perform. Of course, this was an oversimplification, and the process was circular rather than linear. Every time a new person joined the group or there was a new direction, the cycle repeated itself. And when there were people from different companies trying to come together as one unit, things were even more complex.

A lot of teams at Martech seemed to be storming right now; it was competition for power, typical after a major change. It would eventually settle down for a time. Sarah was getting a lot of calls for help with conflict resolution. Mike's group was having a hard time agreeing on a set of procedures. Worse, two of her clients, senior managers, had stopped speaking to one another, and their teams were like gangs preparing for a "rumble." Sarah didn't think gangs had rumbles anymore (that was the Sharks and the Jets in West Side Story, she remembered), but she didn't know what else to call the upcoming meeting between the two sides. Maybe Ed's murder had something to do with the general unrest. Of course, people were upset, though she didn't get the sense that they were grieving for Ed. There had been some stress counselors available early in the week—where did those itinerant soothers come from? And what did they do when there wasn't a school shootings or someone "going postal" (perhaps nobody used that term anymore, either; it might be time to update her slang) and started getting even with everyone who ever looked at him—it was usually a him—the wrong way? Sarah had made a comment to that effect last night. Dev, ever one to keep her honest, sometimes to her irritation, had wondered out loud if she might have wished HR would consult her about this kind of thing rather than automatically call in the outside service. "Dev," she had said, "this kind of thing is not exactly a repeating occurrence. At least, I hope not."

In a way, Roberta had asked her to do something of the sort—not so much to deal with the human stress, but rather the strain on the organization. Sarah promised herself she would call Seth, the journalist, in the morning, though if she sat at her desk long enough, he would surely call her again. With that thought, she got up, grabbed her coat, and pulled on her new rain boots. Classic Wellies, they were, but with polka dots.

Sarah was really looking forward to seeing Alison today. She needed to think out loud. An extrovert, Sarah found that she sometimes didn't know what she was thinking until she said it out loud to someone else. She forced herself to take time to reflect about important issues, but it was a lot easier when she could speak to Alison or Dev about ideas that were only half formed in her mind.

After several days of beautiful autumn-like weather, it was now raining very hard. In the Bay area, nobody was allowed to complain about the rain; after many years of drought and terrible water short-ages, people were expected to say how great it was that it was starting early or continuing late, and how it meant there would be a good snow pack for skiing this winter, or that there wouldn't be a drought this year. If you griped about it, you were in for a lecture.

She scrunched over to the hotel bar across the street in her new boots, which didn't fit all that well but had the attractive quality of keeping her feet dry. Alison hadn't arrived yet. Sarah ordered for both of them; she knew Alison's taste in wine rather well by now—something red and intense; a Shiraz, perhaps, or a zinfandel. The wine arrived before Alison did, and Sarah had to decide whether or not to start drinking hers. This was pretty close to work, after all, and she didn't want to give a passing client the impression that she was a serious solo drinker—especially when there were two glasses in front of her.

Just as she was about to give in and take a sip, Alison arrived, wet and apologetic. She slipped out of her chic but voluminous black raincoat, revealing a tight-fitting deep blue sheath dress with a three-quarter length black military-style jacket. Today's earrings were made of jet; they nearly reached her shoulders. Alison had suffered under the unspoken but harshly enforced dress code at Martech. She had cel-ebrated her change of venue with a trip to Goodwill, accompanied by Sarah, to deposit several large bags of business suits. She hoped there were a lot of tall, size-14 women in the Bay area who would have had successful job interviews in her Martech duds by now.

Alison picked up the glass of wine and swirled it approvingly. She explained that her major client had been with her in a meeting all day. "He kept dithering about our approach to an ad campaign until I was ready to throttle him. Two days of my time this week! And it's not even that big a deal."

"He just can't get enough of you," Sarah teased. This man had been a candidate—in Alison's mind only—for another role in her life until she realized he was married. Or gay. (Maybe both, it had been possible for gay people to marry in San Francisco for a little while and perhaps it would be again.) Naturally, had things been otherwise, she would have passed the account on to someone else at the agency.

"Never dip your pen in the company inkwell; that's what my old mentor always told me," replied Alison.

Sarah laughed. She hadn't heard that saying for some time, and it brought back a memory of a restaurant called *The Company Inkwell* that she had gone to in the Washington, D.C., area long ago with an older male colleague. He was obviously expecting to do some pen-dipping, but that hope was not to be fulfilled. She told the story to Alison. "I left after the salad course, not wishing to be dessert."

As they laughed, Sarah suddenly connected this to what she had learned about Jen and Ed earlier in the week. She leaned forward and touched her friend's arm. "Alison, what would you do if someone told you something that might be relevant to a murder investigation— something that she hadn't told the police?" *Oops.* Sarah had not meant to reveal the gender of her informant. She was rather old-fashioned about English and a stickler for correct usage, even informally. She could never bring herself to use "they" or "them" as an all-purpose pronoun. English was missing that neutral term.

Alison pushed away the plate of nibbles that had come with the drinks. Her body type would have been very fashionable a century earlier; she constantly tried to tame it to fit the leaner and meaner current styles, but with little success. "It would depend on how I felt about the person, I suppose. If it was a confession, I would have to say something, but if it was fairly innocent, or at least not damning, I would probably encourage her to tell the cops herself." Alison swirled the wine in her glass for a moment, then got right to the point. "Who do you think did it?"

"Well, there seem to be more candidates for that role than I first expected. The victim was my client, but I'm finding out that there was a lot I didn't know about him. I guess I have a preferred culprit, but he had nothing to gain and a lot to lose from this guy's death. And the person with most to gain is someone I like. I don't believe this person would be capable of such a thing, but I don't have anyone else in mind." The truth of this had just come clear to Sarah. She really hoped that Jen was not the guilty party—but clearly, at the moment, she appeared to have the strongest motive.

Sarah left the bar with a heavy heart, unlike on most Thursdays.

CHAPTER 13

January 27

It had been two weeks since they had found Ed's body. John had called once or twice to see if she had any "insights" for him. He was always very polite and made sure she had his number "just in case anything occurs to you." John told her that they had confirmed the cause of Ed's death:; strangulation. With his own necktie. At the time she learned this, she had the odd thought that this seemed appropriate. For a Martech employee, that is.

Sarah picked up the phone to call Seth. In his last message, he had said that he was working on his exposé of Martech and that he hoped to interview her to check his facts. Sarah was all for fact checking; she wondered whether anyone but the few remaining big newspapers did it any more. She hoped it would not take a long time, as her work had gotten very intense. While there had been a few days of disruption in the company immediately after Ed's death—hushed voices in the cafeteria, speculation about the guilt or innocence of various senior managers—the wound seemed to have healed over rather rapidly. The calls for her help with resolving team or individual conflicts were back to the usual level. Life had essentially returned to normal. Arthur was named Acting Manager of the department, much to Jen's (and Sarah's) disgust. Maybe Sarah should try to get some time with Roberta again to discover why she had made that choice—but it didn't seem appropriate for her to initiate the conversation. She heard from Jen that Arthur had been on good behavior so far.

Sarah pressed the callback button. Fortunately, Seth's cell phone went right through to voice mail. She left a message suggesting a brief chat early next week.

Today, Sarah had a coaching appointment with a client on the thirty-third floor. It was actually the first time she had been there since her last meeting with Roberta. Passing the conference room, she noticed through the glass wall that Arthur was leading a meeting that included Jen and several of the more junior managers from their groups. As she was heading along the passageway toward her client's office, she heard raised voices coming from the conference room. She recognized Arthur's voice—loud, nasal, and sarcastic—though she couldn't quite make out what he said. She turned back just in time to see Jen storm out of the room, her face red, obviously holding back tears. Sarah hesitated for a moment. Not wishing to embarrass Jen, she decided to continue on her way. She would check in with her later—maybe tomorrow, after she had had a chance to collect herself.

The coaching session went on for longer than usual. Her client, Krish, was preparing for an important meeting with a major customer and wanted to try some approaches out with Sarah to get her feedback and advice. By the time they finished, it was well past five o'clock, the assistants had left, and the light had faded outside Krish's window. His view of the bridge was was somewhat blocked, but at least he had natural light. Sometimes Sarah went for days without seeing the actual outdoors during the working day. Her cubicle was toward the back of the building on her floor, and the windows were on the other side. One had to reach a certain level in this company to have a window to stare out of.

She wished Krish luck, made an appointment to follow up with him to review how the meeting went, then left his office. She walked past the conference room on her way to the elevator. Something seemed odd. The drapes were pulled. That usually happened only when certain very important meetings were held there—meetings where they actually didn't want everyone to know who was attending. The lights were off inside, though. The motion-sensitive lighting was very ecologically correct, though it was embarrassing sometimes when meetings went very quiet and everyone was so bored that there wasn't enough movement in the room to keep the lights on. Sarah was curious, yet a little hesitant. She turned back and saw that Krish had followed her out of his office; she waited a minute for him to catch up.

"Do you think we should open the drapes so people won't be worried in the morning? Everyone is afraid that there may be layoffs once the dust settles from this merger. If the admins see that the room looks prepared for a meeting of the secret cabal, the news will be all over the company in minutes."

"I see what you mean," said Krish in his soft Indian accent. "Maybe the cleaners closed the drapes to vacuum them and forgot to open them again."

They walked to the door of the conference room. Krish opened it briskly, hesitated, and then quickly closed it again. "Don't look," he said to Sarah, who was just behind him and had already seen what he was trying to protect her from. Krish's voice shook. "Someone is in there. Under the table. There's a knife sticking out of his back." He leaned against the now-closed door for support. Sarah, her legs just barely able to carry her, ran back to Krish's office to call 911, forgetting the cell phone in her hand. She had little doubt about who it was under that conference table. The backstabber had been stabbed in the back. She pressed the numbers, holding on to her chest as if that would keep her heart from hammering.

"Someone has been killed...Martech...thirty-third floor. Conference room." Her breathing became more regular as she gave her name and the address. "I will wait by the elevators to direct them."

Sarah looked down at the phone in her hand, as if it had suddenly materialized there. She called Alison to tell her that Girlfriend Thursday would have to be postponed.

CHAPTER 14

January 27

After the necessary work had been done—photograph and study the body, remove it, inspect and seal the room—the interviews began. John had spent an hour or so debriefing Krish, who had a little information, and then Sarah, who had more than she wished she had. "There were five people there in addition to Arthur Antonelli. Jennifer Boehm, Henry Liu, Kristen Nelson, Jeffrey Silverman, Sandip Rao. Jennifer has just begun reporting to Arthur, the others are project leaders on her team or his. They were meeting to discuss something about the merger." Sarah did not volunteer her fleeting observation of Arthur's behavior or her perception of Jen's state of mind; only that she saw her leaving the meeting, perhaps for the lady's room, she speculated to John. That was honest, she was fairly sure that was where Jen had been headed to calm herself down.

Back in her office to gather her belongings, Sarah assumed that John and his partner were now engaged in questioning Jen and the others. She called Dev to say she was on her way home. She had reached him before her interview to say she would be later than usual and why before he started to make dinner.

After her call, Dev had pulled out some cold chicken and made a quick salad that would be ready when she got there. It was after nine when Sarah got home. Her face was flushed and her hair disheveled as she opened the door after turning her key the wrong way twice. "I had not thought that you were going into a dangerous line of work when I agreed to be the househusband," he said wryly as he handed her a drink. "I thought the only crime involving consultants was that they stole your watch so they could tell you what time it is." It was an old and feeble joke, but it broke the tension. Dev hugged Sarah; he was more demonstrative than usual tonight.

"I did have an odd feeling as I walked by that conference room, when I heard the tone of Arthur's voice and saw Jen's face." She was naming names now; she needed a confidante, and there was no one more trustworthy than Dev. "I thought I must have some of the story behind the situation, but I just couldn't put it together, and other things crowded out the sort of informal plan I had made to learn more. I'm a complete failure as a detective—no real strategy or persistence. I will really hate myself if it turns out that I knew something that might have prevented this."

Dev was philosophical. "At least you know that Arthur was not responsible for Ed's death."

"Not really." Sarah's voice was low. "There could be two killers—maybe the two murders are connected, but not by the same hand. I never really thought Arthur was much of a suspect; it seemed to me that he had too much to lose without Ed. As it turned out, though, Roberta was willing to appoint him to Ed's job, so perhaps I was wrong."

Sarah ruffled the fur of the large gray ex-alley cat who had just thudded onto her lap. Oliver evidently thought he was still a tiny kitten, though he must have weighed in at nearly twenty pounds. He had a kind of grating purr, like the motor of an old car that needed a tune-up.

"Maybe someone is trying to make Jen look bad," suggested Dev, beginning to clear the table. "She certainly seemed to be in the wrong place at the wrong time."

That struck Sarah as wishful thinking. She had nearly accepted the fact that Jen was the only likely person to have both the motive and the opportunity to kill Arthur. And it was she who had mentioned backstabbing. "I think I will have to beard the lioness in her den tomorrow, if she is there."

"Be careful," was all Dev had to say in response.

CHAPTER 15

January 28

Jen was not, in fact, there. Her assistant was evasive when Sarah called. Something about being called out to a meeting. Sarah thought she knew what kind of a meeting it would be.

The phone on Sarah's desk rang off and on all morning; it was hard to get anything done. Most of the calls were just to talk over what had happened. The stress people were apparently getting more business this time; several people postponed appointments with Sarah without giving a reason. Their voices had a nervous, edgy tone. Sarah found herself with a block of free time in the afternoon, which was quite unusual. She ignored the ringing phone, guessing it was Seth. She was very grateful that he did not have her mobile number. When it stopped ringing, she made an excuse to call Krish, suggesting that she had some kind of new insight about his approach. Would he like to chat about it? He would. That gave Sarah a reason to head for the thirty-third floor.

She arrived a few minutes early and stopped by Penny's desk. *The poor woman has had a number of shocks lately*, Sarah thought. Still, Penny wore her usual professional demeanor, as if nothing more devastating than a bad quarter had occurred. *Perhaps a bad quarter would be worse, from her point of view*, mused Sarah. The top admins were given a fair amount of company stock. "How are you doing, Penny? You have had a lot to cope with," she understated.

Penny forced a thin smile. "They told me there would be days like this." She glanced longingly at her computer. Sarah took that as a signal to finish the conversation quickly.

"I doubt that Heald Business College had a course that covered this kind of situation," Sarah said. "What is the impact on you with all of this?"

Sarah didn't expect an emotional answer, and she didn't get one. "I was already doing a lot of Ed's work and was very glad when Arthur stepped in—well, I would have preferred Jen." Here she stopped momentarily. This was information she would normally have kept to herself as part of her own professional code. So she was more stressed than she looked. She went on. "I was helping Arthur get up to speed with everything. His old assistant was no help at all." Penny's expression fell somewhere between a disapproving frown and a self-satisfied smile.

All was never exactly well among the impeccably groomed, well-paid assistants. There were old rivalries, current competition for open jobs, cliques. It was understood by everyone in the company that they had far more power than their titles might suggest. They had the ears of the most senior people in the organization and knew how to use their influence. In fact, Sarah supposed that Penny had used her influence to stay with her current job. It was probably no accident that Arthur hadn't chosen to bring his former assistant along with him as might have been expected.

"Was Arthur creating a good transition, do you think? It had to be a challenging situation."

Penny pursed her lips, pausing before she spoke. "I suggested to him—very subtly, of course—that he needed to treat Jen and her group especially carefully. There was a lot of potential for them to sabotage his plans if they thought he was being unfair."

"And do you think he followed your advice?" Sarah was being very careful here—she had gone pretty far out on thin ice by now—but she was saved by the cliquishness.

"My friend Meredith, Jen's assistant, said they were raring for a big fight with Arthur." A ghost of a smile flickered across Penny's face. Meredith was new, a protégée of Penny's. She was very much in Penny's pocket; everything Meredith knew, Penny was sure to hear about sooner or later. "I could not tell Arthur that, of course. But Arthur always thought he could handle any situation, so I don't think it would have made any difference if I had said something. And, of course, now it won't."

"Well," Sarah glanced at her watch. "I need to meet with Krish. It was good to see you. And I'm sorry."

Penny looked at Sarah intently for a moment. "Oh, thanks. I'm fine." She turned toward her computer and began to type. Sarah may as well have faded into the beige carpet. *You might be out of a job, though*, Sarah thought. Whoever took Arthur's job next might have his or her own preferred assistant—or they might find Penny's recent history of losing her bosses a bit off-putting.

The rest of the week went by in a blur. Sarah knew that a lot of police work was going on. Perhaps she would learn about some of it; she was scheduled to see John on Monday. In the meantime, she concentrated on supporting her clients and conducting some stress management sessions. Her own stress would be relieved considerably, she thought, by her upcoming ski weekend with Dev.

CHAPTER 16

February 1

It was Monday and John would be back. Sarah had booked the small conference room for the afternoon. After a weekend of early skiing—at least all the rain had meant that the resorts at Tahoe were going to do well this year—Sarah was feeling reasonably relaxed, though the traffic on their return was atrocious, exactly what one would expect on the first decent ski weekend of the season. On the bright side, it had given Sarah and Dev a chance to talk over the events of the previous week.

Sarah had put the Martech saga strictly out of her mind for most of the weekend. They had borrowed a friend's house very close to both the lake and their favorite ski resort. The crisp air and physical exertion had made her sleep well; and by the time they passed Sacramento on the way home, she was ready to talk. Through patient listening and the occasional probing question, Dev had helped Sarah focus on some key points. She imagined them in Power Point form—when did she start thinking in Power Point? she wondered.

The Martech Murders

- Merger going badly
- Jen and Arthur in competition for Ed's approval, Arthur winning
- Roberta considering firing Ed
- Ed calling me

- Ed strangled with own tie
- Roberta appointing Arthur
- Arthur verbally abusing Jen in meeting
- Arthur found dead in conference room

Viewed that way, it didn't look any better for Jen.

Earlier in the day, Sarah had gone to the twenty-third floor, where Jen's group worked. She stepped into the break room, made a cup of tea, and sat down at the small table. Before long, she was joined by Henry Liu, one of Jen's senior project leaders. Henry had been in that last meeting with Arthur. He greeted Sarah warmly. "I'm glad to see you. Everybody is on *spilkes* around here." It always amused Sarah to hear Henry use Yiddish expressions; he had grown up in New York and had worked his way through CUNY moving racks of clothing around the Garment District.

"It's been a scary time. I'm sure everyone's feeling it. Is Jen back this morning?" asked Sarah.

"She is, but hasn't been down yet. We have a meeting scheduled for this afternoon. I'm worried about her." Henry added milk to his coffee, hesitated, then stirred in some sugar substitute and brought it to the table. He sat down and shook his head slowly.

Sarah nodded encouragingly, hoping he would go on. "She called me over the weekend; seemed very shaken. Of course, we all were," Henry added, as an afterthought.

"You were in that last meeting, Henry. I gather it wasn't a pleasant one." Sarah hoped Henry wouldn't ask her how she knew that. He didn't.

"No. We weren't surprised. Arthur had been fairly quiet since he was appointed, but as you probably know, he's—er, was—a screamer. I guess he finally felt comfortable enough to go back to type last week. He accused Jen of sharing information with the Staticon leaders. He said she was trying to sabotage his plans. He strongly implied that he would tell Roberta that we were all disloyal and not to be trusted." Henry shook his head.

"That must have been distressing. How did the meeting end?"

"Jen defended us, of course. She kept her cool. After a while, Arthur said that the meeting wasn't getting anywhere and ended it rather abruptly."

"Did Jen stay to follow up with him?" Sarah thought she knew the answer to the question, and, to her disappointment, she was right. "Yes, when Kristen and I left, Jen stayed. I think she was trying to persuade him to call you, actually. I heard her say that she thought they needed someone neutral to come in and facilitate a discussion."

"That must have been about midafternoon, then. I passed the conference room around two-thirty and noticed you were pretty deep in discussion." Sarah wondered if her comment sounded inappropriate—what business was it of hers, after all, what time the meeting ended?

Henry didn't seem to notice anything amiss and responded quickly. "I think it must have been around three, since I got back to my cubicle in time for a birthday celebration for one of my team members."

"I hope Jen was able to make it back for that. I know it means a lot to people when the bosses show up at these things." Sarah made an effort to sound casual.

Henry looked thoughtful for a moment. "Yes, I remember that she was kind of rushed. I'm sure she wanted to make it, and Barney, he's the guy whose birthday it was, just works until four. He has day care pickup duty, so he comes in early and leaves early."

"Did..." Sarah weighed her words carefully. "Did she seem OK, except for being rushed? I mean...it sounds as if that was a rough meeting."

Henry paused, looking first down at his shoes and then at Sarah. Sarah realized she might have just gone a bit too far with her questions. "You know, that policeman asked me the same question. They called Kristen and me back to the office Friday evening. My wife wasn't too happy about that, we had dinner plans with some friends. Why shouldn't she be OK? Jen looks soft, but she's not. She's really tough-minded." Henry's shoulders rose as he defended his boss.

"Yes," Sarah said hurriedly. "That has always been my impression of her. Tough, but fair and reasonable." Henry's shoulders relaxed. As far as Sarah knew, Henry, like everyone else on the team, was very grateful to Jen for creating a supportive and challenging climate with many opportunities for learning and career growth. Sarah fervently wished other managers in the company were more like Jen in this respect. She said good-bye to Henry and headed for the cafeteria. She needed to fortify herself before meeting with John, and today was pizza day.

CHAPTER 17

February 1

"Hello, John. I hope you managed to get a break over the weekend. Pretty soon people will think you work here." Sarah said, smiling. She was hoping that John would have no reason to spend much more time here.

"Break? What's that?" John stretched his legs. As long as he had to investigate a murder, he preferred this environment to the grittier ones where he usually spent his time—the Tenderloin, upper Market Street. Everything was slowly gentrifying in The City, but too slowly to suit John, who was something of a clean freak. Someday a mayor would come along who would actually keep his or her promise to deal with the homelessness problem. It was electoral magic, but not so easy to accomplish.

Sitting now in this attractive small conference room on a comfortable chair, with a partial view of the Bay and an interesting witness who was not a suspect, he felt relaxed and almost happy in his work. Work, he reminded himself, which was only what he was going to do until he finished law school. "I wondered what you might have noticed last week, Sarah," he began. "I know we discussed the actual event last Friday, but I was hoping that you might have had some time to reflect on what might have led up to that meeting."

To that murder, you mean. Sarah did not say this aloud, but that was what he was asking, all right. "I don't know much, really." Sarah spoke slowly. She couldn't solve this one herself; not only was it not in her job description, it was also not in her kit bag of competencies.

Maybe she could accomplish more in helping the organization get through this terrible time by collaborating with John. But what did she know that he didn't? What did Roberta really want her to do or say, and where should she draw the line?

"I can't say that I saw it coming, but you know how big organizations are." It suddenly occurred to her that he probably did not. The corporate world was, she assumed, not his usual beat. "I mean, there is always conflict and competition. That's the name of the game. But in the best organizations, that is mostly turned outward, so the company is aligned against competitors."

"And in this organization?" John was sharp. He might have the makings of a good OD consultant. Sarah was often approached by people who were interested in her field. When she met someone who seemed to have the right attitude and skill sets, she sometimes served as a mentor. Many people, though, were not suited to it, and Sarah often felt she had to try gently to dissuade them before they committed to an expensive graduate program. She didn't think John was interested, but his ability to ask good questions, delve deeper, and wait patiently for a response were some of the key abilities needed for the job. She was rather amused to find herself on the other side of that kind of interaction for a change.

"Well, things are a little out of balance right now because of the merger."

"Tell me about that." Damn! He was using her own tricks for drawing people out on her. It worked, too.

"About six months ago, Martech acquired a smaller company in the same industry. It takes a long time to complete the transition. First, there's the due diligence and all the legal and financial stuff; then comes the really hard part, where you have to merge systems like information and communication and all the HR bits like comp and benefits and...do you really need all the details?"

She saw that his eyes had glazed over a bit; he had stopped making notes. "I didn't think so. Well, after all that is done, or at the same time, you still have to figure out who is going and staying.

There's always a lot of duplication, so some people will lose their jobs. That's the most painful part for everyone."

John's posture changed. He was alert again. "Was that going on in the meeting you saw?" he asked.

"I don't actually know. It could have been. I think you talked with Henry Liu; didn't he tell you about the meeting?"

"He didn't mention that. Just that they were discussing how to handle the reorganization after the completion of the merger. I suppose that would be part of it, yes? Would any of the four other people besides Mr. Antonelli have been likely to lose his or her job?"

"I doubt it," Sarah said, although she had no real proof of that. She took a deep breath and decided to share—carefully—some of what she had been thinking about.

Around four o'clock that afternoon, she finally answered a call from Seth. He told her that he was standing right outside the building. Rather than invite him up to her office, she agreed to meet him in the lobby coffee shop. That was about as much intimacy as she thought it right for Seth to have with her or with the company. Stepping off the elevator, she scanned the people sitting at the café tables. Most of them looked corporate. Her eyes lighted on the outlier. Seth looked to be about fourteen (but then, many working people seemed to Sarah these days to resemble high school students). Based on his apparel, she wondered if his day job was as a bike messenger. He had a bag slung across his shoulder, out of which he quickly plucked a camera and flashed it in her face.

It was all Sarah could do to keep from snatching it out of his hand and frog-marching him to the exit after deleting her photo. Instead, she dropped her voice to its lowest register and said, "What would you like to know?"

Seth put on his best investigative journalist face, looking up at her as if from under a trilby hat, and asked, "What kind of an organization harbors a murderer in the executive suite and then tries to keep everything out of the media? How are you involved in the cover-up?" His voice, as she had noticed on his messages, was scratchy and nasal, as if he were about to come down with a cold. Sarah coughed to stop herself from laughing. Seth evidently had been seeing too many mid-twentieth-century movies starring brave young reporters. He was probably her daughter's age and not nearly as sophisticated.

"Seth, I am happy to answer any questions I can, if you are seeking information, but I can't respond to accusations. You would probably get better results as a journalist if you let your curiosity, rather than your desire for sensationalism, drive your interviews." Sarah sat back and waited.

Somewhat to her surprise, Seth grinned. "Touché." They both relaxed. "Seth Vogelsang, boy reporter," he introduced himself. "I work for a web media start-up here in The City. I happened to notice that the mainstream media was basically just offering the party line—stuff that I assume came out of your PR department. I thought we could do better."

Sarah narrowed her eyes. "Just what are you thinking of as 'the party line'?"

"Oh, you know. The company is doing everything it can to cooperate with the police, they are shocked and saddened, they are supporting the family and adding extra protection for the employees. But that's just boilerplate. They would say that if someone had a laptop stolen. I need something real. Otherwise, I'll have to make some educated guesses about what's going on." Seth sat back, squinted, and folded his arms, looking for all the world as if he had an unfiltered cigarette hanging from the corner of his mouth.

Sarah chose to ignore the threat. She told him as little as she reasonably could. He seemed satisfied; perhaps simply having established contact would make him look good. She was sure he would be back.

Later, as she and Dev discussed her day (they had not, she realized, discussed *his* day for some time), she summarized the conversation with John. "I told him broadly about the differences in style and point of view between Arthur and Jen. I discussed the possibility that the top people who had come over from Staticon might get a package that would make it attractive for them to disappear and never create or sign on with a competitor. I even went so far as to mention that I thought Ed might have been on Roberta's short list for a similar package, though I didn't quote her. I did say that I was quite sure it was out of character for Jen to be a backstabber—literally or figuratively. He asked me who else might have an interest in Ed's...and Arthur's job, and I didn't have an answer, other than Jen. I'm pretty sure that this was about more than just a job or a petty internal conflict. Someone must have had a really intense issue with one or both of them, something more personal. Something that was deeply threatening."

Dev responded, somewhat crassly, "Well, I hope whoever it is has solved his or her problem. I'd look forward to an evening with you where we can talk about...oh, politics, or religion, or something innocuous like that."

Dev and Sarah lived on opposite sides of the street when it came to either topic; Sarah came from a non-practicing Berkeley Jewish family. Her father, the labor lawyer, had been a "red diaper baby" whose parents were proud Communists. He was not quite so far to the left, but his legacy to Sarah was an open, questioning mind and a dissatisfaction with the status quo. Dev, on the other hand, was raised as a strict Roman Catholic; he attended parochial school and thought about becoming a priest—until he discovered girls. As an adult, he had strayed from his family's working-class Democratic habits and become a "socially liberal and economically conservative" Republican. Not that there was any room for him in the California Republican Party, which was extremely conservative.

"I think," Sarah ignored Dev's comment, knowing she would have to make it up to him at some point, "I think I had better talk with Roberta tomorrow."

CHAPTER 18

February 2

Roberta's symmetrical features looked composed. If you did not notice the tic somewhere behind her left eye, you might have thought she was relaxed. Tom brought in a pot of tea and some elegant china cups. As a tea drinker, Sarah really appreciated the ceremony as well as the flavor. Lady Grey was Roberta's favorite. Sarah spelled it "favourite" in her mind; it was such a delicate British tea. She herself usually preferred something a little bolder and more straightforward, like the workman's "cuppa" that she had learned to drink with milk on her first trip to England, but this would be fine today. "How are you doing with all of this, Roberta?" A gentle prod.

"I can tell you, Sarah, that I am a nervous wreck. I am supposed to hold it all together—and I have been, for the sake of the department—but when you called today, I was so glad to know that there was someone I could let my hair down with."

A moderately amusing picture of sleek Roberta with long curls popped into Sarah's mind. *Stop it*, she thought. This was as close as Roberta had ever come to expressing the usual human emotions, at least to Sarah. She must be terribly upset, Sarah thought, to say this much—though she looked, as she usually did, serene and composed.

"I have no idea what to do now. The work has to continue. Someone has to take over the reins of the department, but the only obvious person right now is Jen, and I think she's too distracted. She knows that a lot of people are suspicious that she had something to do with...well, at least with Arthur's death."

"Are you?" Sarah tried to make the question sound innocent.

"Well…I certainly didn't think she had anything to do with Ed's death." There was a faint emphasis on "Ed." That was damning with faint praise, indeed, thought Sarah. Roberta continued, "But I knew that she and Arthur didn't get along. I was a bit concerned when I appointed Arthur to Ed's position temporarily, but frankly, I felt that he needed a new start, whereas Jen was doing extremely well with her team; and I didn't want to jeopardize their coherence just when it's most needed."

Sarah was a little taken aback by this explanation. It made some sense, but if that was true, why didn't Roberta take Jen into her confidence? Arthur's appointment must have felt like a slap in the face to Jen. "So you are concerned that if you appoint Jen now, others might feel that you were following the script of someone who was…not exactly neutral in the situation?"

"That is a very diplomatic way to put it, Sarah. If Jen is the…I mean, if she had anything to do with this, then I can't be seen as colluding with her." Roberta had not risen to her position by taking great risks, Sarah thought. She gave a quick summary of her discussions with John and her meeting with Seth. Roberta thanked her and did not ask any follow-up questions.

Sarah stopped by Tom's desk as she left Roberta's office. He was carefully kitted out, as usual. Tom did not subscribe to the Staticon culture's "anything is business casual as long as it covers your butt" mantra. She was sure Tom looked good in shorts, but she was equally certain that she would never have the opportunity to enjoy the view. "How does she seem to you?" he asked, a little anxiously. The admins tended to have much higher emotional intelligence than their bosses. Of course, they had to in order to read their minds—one of the requirements of the job. Tom was clearly aware of Roberta's stress and concerned about it.

"I think she's all right, Tom, just worried. I'm sure that if things quiet down…" (by which she meant no more murders) "…she will be as good as new in no time."

Sarah realized that was a cliché, and she was annoyed with herself. "Tom," she remembered to ask, "Did you notice anything unusual last Friday? Were either Jen or Arthur in Roberta's office earlier in the day?"

Tom's face closed up as if a light had been snapped off. "Nothing unusual," he replied. In the old days, they were called confidential secretaries. They got paid for keeping secrets. Sarah had clearly over-stepped a boundary. Again. If she were going to do this detective thing, she would really have to be a lot more subtle about it.

CHAPTER 19

February 4

It was late Thursday afternoon. The rest of the week had been quiet, at least on the thirty-third floor. She had not heard anything from John, but she was sure there was a lot going on behind the scenes. Seth kept calling, asking for another meeting, which she put off. Jen had been in and out but somehow never available to meet; they now had a date for tomorrow afternoon, but Sarah didn't have high expectations that it would happen. The organization seemed to be getting on rather well without Arthur—something that would have pained him to know, she thought. Several of her clients managed to have emergencies at once: internecine squabbles, loss of a key contributor to a competitor. Chantal, one of her newer clients, called her for help in preparing a presentation for an executive board meeting. Chantal intrigued Sarah; she was a brilliant, statuesque African American woman, as tall as Alison and exceptionally beautiful, with high cheekbones and ebony skin. She seemed very confident, but told Sarah openly that she sometimes felt out of her depth with the organizational politics at Martech. Sarah enjoyed coaching Chantal; she was a quick learner and looked to have a very good future with the company, if someone didn't snatch her away with a better offer. The day was very busy in a refreshingly ordinary way; three or four emergencies of that type per week were normal for Sarah.

She tossed her phone and keys into her large bag, shrugged into her warm coat, and walked out with a sense of anticipation. It had been two very full weeks since she had caught up with Alison. She felt

fortunate to be married to Dev, a man who actually liked to talk—
even about his feelings, sometimes—and, even better, knew how to
listen. Still, there was something about the close relationship with a
girlfriend that fulfilled other needs; it was as if, by talking about the
minutia of their lives and listening to one another, they became more
real; their experiences took on a more storied, almost heroic aspect.
Sarah smiled at her attempt to describe the indescribable; she had
missed her friend last week and looked forward to seeing her now.

Alison glided into the bar wearing one of her "rigs," as she liked to
call them. Gaucho pants and a bolero; a sort of unisex tango outfit—
though nobody would have mistaken Alison for a gaucho, especially
given the flaming red low-cut shirt beneath the bolero. She greeted
Sarah with a light kiss on both cheeks. Alison had spent some time
in France as a young woman and came to like this form of greeting.
It did not seem pretentious, but Sarah sometimes forgot with Alison
or when traveling in Europe herself whether it was right-then-left or
the other way around; she always worried about a potential collision.
They settled down and ordered their wine and some nibbles. Alison
had to catch Sarah up on her latest boyfriend, Larry. Sarah had only
recently learned about him. "Can you believe it? First he invited me
and then he *uninvited* me to the show at the A.C.T. Said he only could
buy six tickets, and his other daughter's boyfriend showed up; and
with his ex-wife, her husband, and the three of them, he had to leave
me out. And then he had the nerve to call me from an above-ground
stop at BART and ask which station was closest to the theater!" Alison tossed her head of remarkably chestnut hair—she had a good
colorist.

"He's not the perfect boyfriend for you," said Sarah.

"Oh, that's where you're wrong. He's exactly perfect for me. He
is an engineer. That doesn't do much in the emotional intelligence
department—maybe a little Asperger's thrown in—but he can fix
anything. Plumbing, electrical, broken furniture—everything. And
he's good in bed. I am so not interested in getting married anymore,
Sarah. He's just unreliable enough to keep me from wanting to—but
he still will come over if something breaks. Perfect, as I said."

Sarah laughed; then they caught it from one another and had a very undignified case of the giggles. Two middle-aged women, laughing until they practically fell out of their chairs, and they hadn't even finished one drink. *Well, there you are*, thought Sarah, gasping for breath. *You just don't do this with a guy.*

Sarah told Alison (without using names, of course) the latest about the saga of Martech. As she spoke, she realized that her amateur sleuthing hadn't gotten her very far. If she had a talent for getting to the truth—and her clients had always told her that she did—she wasn't using it very well in this situation. All the signs pointed to Jen, who had both the motive and the opportunity, but Sarah was sure it was not in her character to do something like that. *It is just too trivial an excuse for such a desperate act. I can see Arthur driving Jen to drink, but not to kill. And Ed almost seems lost in this whole picture now; why would anyone want to kill him? Oh, of course, Jen's team wasn't surprised by it...but still...*

"Alison," she asked abruptly, "what would drive you to kill your boss?"

"Let me count the reasons." Alison held up one hand and made an enumeration gesture.

"No, I really mean it. What might he or she do that would be so terrible, so threatening, that you wouldn't just wash your hands of the whole thing and go after another job—or start a rival firm?"

"Well...if he knew something that would send me to jail for life...or if he turned out to be an ax murderer himself and I was saving the world from him...or if he hurt a member of my family..." Alison trailed off. There really weren't that many motives. If one was a normal, reasonable person, that is....

CHAPTER 20

February 5

To Sarah's surprise, Jen was in on Friday morning, and they agreed to meet for a "walk-and-talk" around eleven o'clock. The weather had done its usual San Francisco winter trick and might have passed for spring anywhere else. As they walked along the Embarcadero, Sarah opened the conversation gently by asking how things were going.

"About what you would expect," said Jen. "Nobody has actually accused me of anything, but it's pretty clear that I should not be leaving town any time soon." She forced a wry smile. "My team is treating me like an invalid. I expect to see a large bowl of chicken soup on my desk any day now. We are getting work done, though. I suppose I shouldn't say this, and I trust you won't quote me, but it's a lot easier to get the resources we need than it was before. Roberta just says yes to everything we ask for. I'm not sure she even thinks about it. We even have permission to hire Lee—if we can get his visa approved."

"That sounds good," Sarah temporized. She slowed her stride a little, and Jen followed her lead. "You know, with all the focus on Arthur, I haven't thought much about Ed. I guess you knew him better than anyone else at Martech."

"In the biblical sense, you mean?" Jen said drily. "Actually, I doubt that. Ed was quite the ladies' man—or so he thought. I'm sure that in the time he was at Martech he broke a few hearts, or at least a few homes. He preferred married women. Less trouble-making potential. I was an exception."

"Was your relationship…serious?" Sarah was surprised at how open Jen was being with her and wanted to push it just a little.

"I thought it was. From the time we first worked together at that company, he claimed that he was separated from his wife. We were often together on business trips, and…things happened. We shared a lot of interests and had the same sense of humor; that has always been a strong draw for me. I was quite young then, and I believed his stories…and the feelings he expressed for me."

"What finally happened?"

"Well, he had a skiing accident and was hospitalized. His wife picked up his belongings, including his phone. I guess she must have suspected something, because she checked his text messages. She found several from me, along with his responses—they weren't exactly work-related. And when she called me later, she made sure that I knew that she had found similar messages to three other women."

Sarah lifted an eyebrow. "They remained together, though."

"They did then. I think it was largely for financial reasons. They finally split up last year; she decided to marry her psychiatrist." That probably left his ex-wife out as a suspect, thought Sarah. She had initiated the divorce and was presumably happier because of it.

"You've stayed in touch with her, then." Sarah was breathing hard. Jen slowed her pace a little to allow Sarah to catch up.

"Just now and then. When she somehow learned that I was working for Ed again, she sent me a condolence card. Meant to be funny, I guess."

"How did that come about?" This had been puzzling Sarah. Why would Jen volunteer to work for someone who had messed up her life so thoroughly?

"It was all business, really. He came to the company around the same time I did by coincidence, and we had occasional polite contact. I had no hard feelings by then; I had chalked it up to experience. It made me much more careful about relationships, especially with colleagues. When he had an opening that he felt could be right for me, he called, and that was that. He did have respect for my skills, and he never tried to recreate our former relationship. We found a comfortable way of working together; I was quite happy with the way things were going. Recently, though, he has...had become quite distant, less supportive. You knew that, of course, because of the visa issue we discussed."

"Yes." Sarah did not want to pursue that topic at the moment. "What was your sense of the relationship Ed had with Roberta?"

"Well, I'm pretty sure it wasn't romantic, if that's what you mean. Ed would never like...I mean, he always wanted to be the powerful one in the relationship. A younger woman or someone who was junior to him, that was more his style."

"I meant as a boss," Sarah said, though she was glad to have the additional information.

"Oh, I think he just put up with her. He sucked up to anyone in power, but I am pretty sure he had his eye on her job."

"What about the reverse? What did she think about him?"

"Well, Roberta certainly never confided in me—she keeps her own counsel—but I don't think he had much of a future with her." This matched the information that Sarah already had from her conversation with Roberta. She wondered how common that knowledge had been.

"What gave you that sense, Jen?"

Jen thought for a minute. Sarah assumed that she was weighing how much to tell her. "There were stories...you know how things get around here. People had been saying that there was a lot of tension between them. Then someone on my team overheard a telephone conversation in the ladies' room—people will answer their phones anywhere now—and Roberta, she was sure it was Roberta, said something like, "If you mention that to anyone, I will know about it, and your career here will be finished."

"What made her think it was Ed she was speaking to?"

"I think it was a matter of elimination—no pun intended. Roberta only had three direct reports other than Tom, and two of them are women. My associate was almost certain she heard a man's voice, though of course she couldn't tell what he was saying. And the conversation stopped, probably when Roberta realized that there was someone nearby." Sarah was skeptical; such a conversation need not have been with a direct report.

Sarah was looking forward to the weekend. As she stepped into her cubicle, she saw that her message light was flashing. Most people she spoke with on a regular basis had her cell number, so a call to her work phone was, more often than not, someone trying to sell her something: external consulting services, training programs, professional society memberships—mostly things she didn't need or had no budget for. Or, of course, it could be Seth. She was tempted to ignore it, finish up some reports that were due, and get home a little earlier than usual. The flashing kept dividing her attention, though, so she decided to check the message just to make it stop.

"Hi, Sarah. It's Bengt." Bengt was the CEO of Staticon, the acquired company. She had met him a few times since the merger. He was tall, blond, very Nordic-looking, but with a strong Boston accent. His father, she remembered hearing, had been a visiting professor at M.I.T. and had decided to stay and raise his family in the U.S. "I wonder if we can talk. If you're free, we could meet for a drink after work."

Sarah sighed. On any other day, the thought of having a drink with this beautiful and interesting man would have been pleasant— as she often said to Alison, she might be married, but she wasn't dead! Of course, she would not have wanted to pursue anything beyond a drink; she had long outgrown the need to test the limits of her relationship with Dev, but she did enjoy the occasional informal social conversations she had with clients or prospective clients. It was often a good way to begin a project or just to have a deeper conversation about their real concerns. She was past the age where she questioned male clients' motives in asking her out for a drink. Today, however, it was not the way she had hoped to begin her evening. Still, Bengt's insights would be new and could be valuable, given that most of the merger meetings she had facilitated were only attended by Martech people. Which was odd, come to think of it. Why would the company being acquired be left out of those planning meetings? Of course, maybe he just wanted to talk about developing his team. *Not likely*, she thought, and reached for the phone to return his call.

CHAPTER 21

February 5

Bengt and Sarah settled into their seats at a corner table at the Hyatt Regency bar. It had had a recent makeover, Sarah noticed. It had gotten a little tatty over the years, but the new and improved bar was quite striking with its curtain of tiny lights and swooping tangerine-colored seating. It seemed as busy as usual with the Friday after-work crowd—at least, those who had not taken off early for the ski slopes.

Bengt had removed his tie (Sarah assumed it was the first place he had worked where a tie was required) and unbuttoned the top button of his starched blue shirt. He wore a plain gold necklace underneath, and Sarah could just see the top of what she assumed was an elaborate tattoo. He got right to the point. "There's something really funny going on in this company. I thought you might have some insight and maybe some advice for me." Bengt's voice was deep and resonant; it carried, though he was clearly making an effort to speak quietly. Sarah, hoping that the meeting would be a short one, did not make her usual encouraging noises, the vocalizations that seemed to free clients to tell her about hopes, fears, grand visions, or conspiracy theories. Things they would normally keep to themselves. Bengt had a head of steam, though, and rolled on. "For the past six months, my team and I have been doing our level best to make this merger work. I thought I had reached an understanding with Ed a few weeks ago as to how we would resolve some outstanding issues. We had developed a plan...we are speaking confidentially, right?" Bengt broke off and looked at Sarah.

"Of course. I'm a little unclear at this point as to whether you want me to take an active role in something or just listen, but in either case, I will consider this conversation confidential."

"Good. I will speak freely then. Ed and I had come up with a plan. Our idea was to make Staticon a semi-autonomous division of the company that would focus on innovation. It just isn't working very well to try to absorb it into the overall corporate culture. We would keep the key talent that way and be able to make a real contribution to Martech's success. We had discussed rearranging the space so that we Staticon people could have two floors to ourselves. We could design them as we wish, and we could operate with our own norms. You might know, for example, that we've always had the same 20 percent rule that Google has. People can use up to that amount of time to work on projects they find interesting without having to have anyone's approval. Some of our best ideas have come from that practice."

"And, I assume, some of your worst ones as well?" Sarah smiled. She was drawn to this approach, but couldn't imagine it working at uptight Martech.

"Not really. The worst ones are generally the things that management or even customers have asked for—they don't know what they don't know, so those ideas are usually just a variation on what we already do; they don't break any new ground."

Sarah was sorry she had stopped Bengt in mid-flight; he was clearly going somewhere with this narrative. "So you were happy with this plan." She wanted to hear more about Ed. He hadn't confided this plan to her at all; she had thought he was leaning toward Arthur's "throw the bums out" solution.

"I was, and so were all the members of my team. We're all still pretty passionate about what we do and not ready to retire and take up golf. Of course, I was stunned when Ed was killed, but I assumed that the plan would go forward. I think it was a day before...the end of Arthur's tenure—" (*What an odd way to put it*, thought Sarah.) "—I got a call from him. He said he'd like to meet to discuss 'packages' for the senior executives on our team. I was shocked. I told him what Ed and I had agreed to, but he said that he was in charge now, and the plans had changed. To be honest, I suddenly wondered if he hadn't been involved in Ed's death—though that would seem like a drastic way to get a promotion. And I don't understand what he would have had to gain by getting rid of us."

Something clicked in Sarah's mind. "I remember hearing that there was some legal problem with one of your products. Might he have been concerned about liability issues? I know that there was some talk about shutting development on it down in order to prevent further damage. And I gathered that you disagreed."

"Yes. This is actually our most innovative and promising product. There were some concerns about patent infringement. Our attorney has assured me that we have an excellent case. The inventor had previously worked for a rival company, and that company claimed that it owned the patent on the underlying technology, but we can prove that this was independently developed after the inventor left that organization."

Sarah was wading in deep water here. Her attorney father had hoped she would follow his career direction, but her interest in the law as a tool for "peace, justice, and the American Way" (her dad liked to quote the old Superman comics, a bit sarcastically) was mitigated by her lack of interest in law school—too many details to focus on; she preferred a big-picture, conceptual approach.

"How do you think I can help?" Sarah was slightly flattered that Bengt had sought her out. She evidently didn't display the stodgy Martech brand on her forehead. At the same time, she was wary about getting too deeply involved in high-level strategic conflicts, as she had neither the technical nor the executive background that might help her gain an understanding of the effectiveness of one strategic direction over another. She did not feel, either, that she had any influence on decisions at that level, other than those involving change management strategies or people issues.

"I'm hoping that with your knowledge of the organization and your ability to communicate...of course, I know you are very discreet…you might be able to give me a sense of which way the winds are blowing. If the agreement that Ed and I made is really dead, then I want to be able to make my plans accordingly, and soon. I do have some new ideas and lots of connections. On the other hand, if it still seems possible, then I will stick it out until the new order is clear. I guess there will be a lot of turmoil until the…'situation'… is resolved, and there is someone new in that role that I can deal with." Bengt made the air quotes gesture when he said "situation." Of course, Sarah knew what he meant.

"Bengt, I really can't share any information with you that I might learn in the course of my job. It would violate all the rules of the road that I have to follow as an internal consultant; it's sometimes called a 'trusted advisor' role, and there is a reason for that." Sarah thought for a moment. She really liked Bengt and all that he represented and thought the deal that he and Ed had proposed was an excellent plan. Maybe there was a way she could help. "If you are OK with not knowing any details, I might be able to signal you if I see that it is a lost cause. That seems fair and is something I could live with."

Clearly, Bengt would have liked more, but he accepted that this was the best Sarah could do for him, and they promised to stay in touch over the next few weeks. They agreed that if Sarah sent him an e-mail or left a message including the words "the chemistry isn't right," he would understand her to mean that he should make the best deal he could and move on. They sealed the agreement with a drink and parted ways.

CHAPTER 22

February 5

"What have I gotten myself into?" Sarah and Dev were settled comfortably in front of the environmentally friendly, but not quite satisfying, gas fireplace in their living room. It gave them the illusion of a crackling fire without the warmth, the delicious odors, or the sounds. The cat liked it, though. He was splayed out in front of it, all four paws in the air in a "dead cat" pose.

"First, I find myself mixed up in two murders, then I agree to be the liaison from the company to the police—as well as to a very green but ambitious journalist—and now I think I just agreed to be an in-house corporate spy."

"You do lead an interesting work life," Dev responded. "My work is extremely boring and predictable in comparison. The geek cabal has not invited me to launch any denial-of-service attacks on foreign governments lately."

Sarah smiled; she knew that Dev enjoyed hearing about the ins and outs of corporate politics and appreciated her skills—but would not have traded places with her for any amount of money. Being his own boss suited him; he was very good at his work; good enough that he could choose the projects that interested him and hand others off to friends who were not quite so much in demand.

"I think I have been letting events get ahead of me. As long as I've been handed a role in this corporate drama, whether I wanted it or not, I had better put my skills to use. So far, I have a lot of inside information that I didn't ask for and a lot of questions based on that information. Maybe it's time for me to do what I do best—treat it as an OD challenge. It's just possible that a consulting intervention sooner rather than later could prevent more trouble." Sarah made a sweeping gesture with the hand that held her wineglass. She quickly put the glass down as the wine came dangerously close to an encounter with the carpet. As often happened, she hadn't known what she was thinking until she was in conversation with someone she trusted. That was how many of her decisions were made. Once she realized that she might be in a position to affect events, she tended to be driven to action.

"Just a thought..." Dev swirled his wine and frowned. "This isn't a matter of a simple internal conflict or political game-playing, Sarah. I mean, you're good, but someone has a major issue here. Two people have been killed. I don't want to see you putting yourself in danger. How do you think you can help resolve this? What can you do that the police can't?" Suddenly very concerned about her safety, Dev seemed to be pulling back the encouragement he had been offering for several weeks.

"A lot. I've been with this company a long time. I understand the relationships and the conflicts. I have a lot of the corporate memory between my ears. That knowledge is important. And I have a set of skills to go with it that might be just what's needed right now. I know how to get people talking, and I know how to listen deeply. I can drill down to the really important information, not just the first thing that people say because they think it's what you want to hear. And I know how to design interventions that facilitate change—ways to get people involved and committed to a new direction. I'm sure that's why John has wanted me to be kind of an internal partner for him, not just a communication channel. I have resisted committing to that role until now, because I couldn't see how I could help without violating my own principles. But after my talk with Bengt today, something clicked into place for me. I think I have the key to understanding some of what is going on, although I don't know what it is yet. I think it has something to do with why Ed called me just before he was murdered. And I mean to find out what it is."

Dev knew better than to try to dissuade Sarah from a course of action, once she had made up her mind. "Just promise me that you will be careful." He looked at her directly, gave her a rather romantic kiss for an old married couple, got up, and asked her to turn off the faux fireplace and come to bed. Sarah grinned and followed him. She felt lighter than she had for some time.

CHAPTER 23

February 12

The second week of February proved to be relatively quiet. Sarah spent several hours coaching Chantal, whose first presentation to the board had gone so well that she was asked to organize a task force of senior managers to develop recommendations for increasing diversity at Martech. Chantal wasn't sure whether she should be pleased or annoyed by the stereotypical nature of the request, but Sarah encouraged her to see it as an opportunity, both to get to know some of the other senior managers better and to become better known herself. If this proved to be a successful venture, she could reasonably ask for another assignment that was less related to her ethnicity and more to her competence. Coaching people like Chantal was one of the things Sarah most enjoyed about her job. She could see the results of her work through the improved skills and increased visibility of these promising young leaders. It gave her some quiet satisfaction to see them grow and make important contributions to the organization.

She got caught up on her paperwork, successfully evaded Seth, enjoyed her time with Alison, and set aside some time on Friday morning to think through the situation, which she had mentally labeled "The Murders on the 33rd Floor." She had decided to treat it as if it were a consulting engagement.

Sarah opened her desk drawer and pulled out a pack of small sticky notes. She would try a mind-mapping technique to help her think through how to proceed. She began to write all the known elements of the system, mentally drawing a line around the system that had resulted in two murders. She wrote one element on each note and then began to arrange them in clusters by category. Doing this always helped her to sense what was missing—gaps in her knowledge or additional elements (people, groups, events, issues) that she hadn't considered at first. She placed these on a large sheet of flip chart paper and began moving them around, looking for relationships and connections, especially non-obvious ones. Both Ed and Arthur, married men at the time, had been attracted to Jen. Was there some competition there? Did Jen have a jealous partner in the background? Penny was single; was she involved with Ed? Might she have a motive for dispatching him? How about Jen's very loyal team members? They were in that last meeting with Arthur. Could they have collaborated in seeing him out? Granted, that would have been carrying loyalty a little far, Sarah mused.

When she had gone as far as she could with this, she folded up the paper and put it in her locked cabinet, as she did with client notes. She would look at it again in a day or so; perhaps more thoughts would have jelled by then. Next, she took another large sheet of paper, turned it to landscape mode, and drew a timeline across it. She hesitated for a moment as to where the timeline started; then, realizing that her entry into the situation was probably some distance into the process, she wrote the date of Ed's call to her about a third of the way across the paper. If she were going to make any sense of this, she needed to know what led up to that call. She entered other known events with dates up to her meeting with Bengt, which she placed about a third of the way from the right-hand edge of the paper, then drew a dotted line up to the edge. She left room both below and above the timeline of her own immediate knowledge for what she might learn that others knew about. Satisfied for now, she placed that paper in the cabinet as well.

Just as Sarah was about to leave her cubicle for another coaching meeting with Chantal, her desk phone rang. It was John. "How are things?" he asked her. "Can we talk soon?" John evidently still thought that she could help him. Well, maybe she could. "How about this afternoon, John? I'm free after three-thirty. Let's meet for coffee in the Starbucks across the street from here."

Sarah was a little out of breath when she arrived at the coffee shop. Her afternoon meeting had been long and fairly productive; and, as often happened, she had lost track of time. John was already halfway through his café latte. He was sitting at one of the few tables, wearing "business casual" clothes today: a polo shirt and tailored slacks. He looked a lot like the middle managers sitting nearby, taking a break. *A master of disguise*, Sarah thought, chuckling to herself. John's face was long, and he had an aquiline nose; he could have belonged to any number of ethnic groups. One day, she would ask where in China his family had come from. She ordered her drink, a nonfat chai latte, and joined him. "John, I don't have anything for you right now, but I wanted you to know that I have started to think more seriously about how I might approach this. I'm going to think of it as a type of consulting engagement. I've started using some of the tools that are helpful to me in my work. I just have one problem…"

"And that is…?"

"I don't know who to think of as my client. That probably sounds odd to people who are not in my profession, but it's important to understand the roles and relationships involved in any engagement. Whose needs should I be focusing on? What are the goals? What kind of agreements should we have with one another? "

"That sounds like serious business, Sarah." John's suppressed smile suggested to Sarah that he, like Dev, found her rules of engagement a little pretentious. "I'll volunteer for that role."

"I don't think so, John. You aren't paying my salary. I'm an internal consultant, remember?" Sarah could hear the irritable edge in her voice. She did not like to be seen as self-important or stuffy, even when she knew she was.

"I don't suppose I could afford you. But let's just say that if you can help me get this resolved and get someone behind bars, your organization is going to be a lot safer place to work."

He had a point.

Sarah told John about the mind map she had developed earlier in the day and asked for his help. "What are the key questions that we need to answer? What things might be easier for me to investigate than for you? I'd like to list them and then think about which ones I can best tackle, and who might have some information or insight on each of them."

John had the information about who was where during the key times; (no strangers had showed up on data from the security cameras positioned near the elevators on the thirty-third floor.) He had already told her that there was no physical evidence left on either murder weapon. Whoever it was had been very careful not to leave tracks. What he didn't understand were the dynamics, the interactions, the relationships, the vested interests. After an hour or so, they had a list:

- *Why did Ed call Sarah in the first place?*
- *Who, besides Jen, had anything to gain from either man's death?*
- *What were the dynamics behind the merger issue? Who had a vested interest in the merger's failure or success?*
- *What hidden issues might there be in the organization that could be related to any of the parties or relationships?*

Sarah agreed to meet John early in the following week and give him a report on what, if anything, she had learned. She had planned to head for home after her meeting with John, but something drew her back to her cubicle. She opened the locked cabinet and pulled out the "mind map." On it were clusters of notes labeled "People," "Groups," "Issues," and "History." She took out her smartphone to snap a photo of that arrangement, then hesitated. While Sarah liked technology and used it frequently and competently, she found this physical mind-mapping technique more useful when she was thinking about a complex system. Moving things around on the paper often helped to create new connections in her mind. She decided to look at another angle: motivation. Oddly, the "seven deadly sins" popped into her mind. Being married to Dev, who considered himself a "recovered Catholic," had given her some familiarity with Catholic theology, at least the version he grew up with; however, her favorite association with the concept came from a meeting she had attended at Apple Computer some years before in a building whose conference rooms were named after the sins. She remembered that the meeting was in Lust, though there was nobody in attendance that tempted her in that particular direction. She wrote the names of each sin on a sticky note, leaving out Gluttony and Sloth, which she doubted were relevant. That left Pride, Avarice, Lust, Envy, and Anger. Each one seemed like a possible motivation for murder. She began moving the names she had generated earlier toward a marker or two that might help her understand the deeper motivations of each player.

Jen—Anger or Envy
Roberta—Pride
Bengt—Anger or Avarice
Penny—Lust or Anger

If she were to include Arthur as a suspect in Ed's murder, Avarice was certainly a possibility. Could Lust or Envy have moved anyone besides those already on her map? Who was missing? Tom? Henry? Her map was clearly not complete. Sarah snapped a photo and decided to leave it as it was over the weekend; she and Astrid had an appointment on Saturday to visit a boutique that specialized in chic mother-of-the-bride dresses. Astrid was managing all aspects of this wedding, and Sarah would certainly not be left to her own devices when it came to appearances.

CHAPTER 24

February 13–15

Much as she loved her daughter, Sarah had been dreading the mother-of-the-bride dress ordeal. In the end, however, it was not as bad as she had feared. Later, relaxing at home while Dev carved the rotisserie chicken he had bought at the market nearby and prepared a salad, she reflected on what she had been afraid of. Astrid's disapproval? Loss of autonomy? Pastels? The wine-colored gown that she and Astrid had agreed on fit beautifully; Sarah could actually imagine wearing it more than once—not that she and Dev had many occasions to dress up. Perhaps the dress would change that. She imagined them appearing at one of the museum balls she dutifully subscribed to and never attended, for fear of not fitting in with the San Francisco *haute monde*.

Suddenly, Sarah sat up straight. Fear! How could she have left that out of her collection of motivators? Fear of loss—it was always one of the most important issues she had to deal with in her conflict resolution engagements. You could not resolve a serious conflict without reducing the fear that kept the parties from being able to come to an agreement. That's why a third party was important; as long as all parties to the conflict trusted that person, he or she could work on reducing the fears each party had of the others. But if the motive for the murders was fear, there had been no third party available. Not for the first time since Ed's call, she felt a twinge of guilt. Had she missed something? Could she have done anything to prevent this if she had been more alert to the signs of hidden conflict?

Sarah got to her cubicle early Monday morning. She wanted to squeeze in a couple of hours of thinking time before her appointments started. She pulled out the mind map she had been working on, placed a sticky note in the upper right-hand corner labeled "Fear," and started to develop associations. Fear of...loss, harm, harm to loved ones (remembering what Alison had said), failure...which fears could lead to murder? She wanted to record all of the underlying fears that commonly showed up in organizational conflict. She elaborated on *loss*. Loss of face, of respect, of status, of a job, of an important relationship. Loss of an argument? Maybe that didn't rise to the level of the others. Most of the conflicts where she was called to mediate or facilitate a resolution or a negotiation involved one or more of the fears she had listed. What might each of the key people she had listed have to lose? And who was she not considering? For that matter, what did she know—and, more importantly, what didn't she know—about the key people?

To learn more, she decided to call on one of her most useful resources, LinkedIn, a social networking site focused on business and professional relationships. She was one of those people with more than five hundred connections, some of whom she had never actually met, but that made it possible for her to meet or learn about people who were connected to her connections. She tried each of the names on her map, including Ed and Arthur, to learn about their work history and some personal details. Most of what she saw was not new to her. She was already connected to many of the people they were connected to. After half an hour, she had learned the following:

- Jen had been born in The Netherlands; that explained the ghost of an accent. Sarah had noticed each time she visited Amsterdam (one of Martech's affiliates was located there) that people in The Netherlands seemed to speak better English than she did.
- Roberta's résumé was oddly brief; there seemed to be a gap between the time she graduated from the University of Florida and the first job that was listed—a senior administrative

position in a large insurance firm. Perhaps she did not want to list lower-level jobs?

- Arthur had worked in two Wall Street firms before moving to the corporate world.
- Tom had gone from his university straight to Martech; he apparently had never worked for another company. He had held two other admin positions in the company before coming to work for Roberta.
- Penny was not on LinkedIn. Sarah checked Facebook and found her, but most of the information on it would be private unless she connected to her, which did not seem appropriate at this point.

It seemed to be true that one's private life was now more public than ever. Sarah was glad that in her own slightly misspent youth, social networks were limited to the people she actually knew—if they had something on her, well, she probably had something on them as well, and the world at large need never know. Of course, the staid site she had been studying was hardly full of revelations; it was designed to attract potential employers and business partners.

It was time to move into the more formally planned part of her day; she had a meeting with Krish and his team for a strategic planning session. As she put things away and prepared for the meeting, Sarah had a sense that something of what she had learned would prove to be useful. She promised herself that she would probe a bit more deeply as soon as she had time.

Seth called again that afternoon. The way he popped up just as she thought he had gone on to something else reminded her of the whack-a-mole game at a fair. She had met with him a few times since their first encounter, each time offering less information. This was a strategy she had learned in a negotiation skills seminar many years ago: if your concessions become smaller and smaller over time, you are likely to complete the deal sooner. She sighed and agreed to another meeting in the downstairs café.

Seth had affected a pencil behind his ear this time; he had an absurdly large notebook open on the table in front of him. What would be next, a green eyeshade? "Sarah, the public is becoming very suspicious. Why is it taking so long to find and arrest the murderer? It must be someone very high up in the organization—I'm sure if it had been a janitor, he or she would be under lock and key by now."

Although Sarah knew that Seth's "public" probably consisted mainly of his Facebook friends, she treated his question politely. She knew that if anything, however absurd, about Martech happened to go viral, the company would have a very difficult time convincing customers and stockholders that it was untrue. It seemed to her that if something was repeated often enough, people began to believe it.

"The police are working very hard on this, Seth. And the company is cooperating fully with the police and the press."

"Then why..." Seth snapped his notebook shut, adjusted his backward baseball cap lower on his forehead, leaned forward, and looked directly into Sarah's eyes. "Why hasn't the internal conflict about the merger come out in the open?"

Sarah deliberately leaned back in the aluminum café chair. She took off her glasses and polished them. Having found her center once more, she spoke calmly. "Seth, that is the company's business. It has nothing to do with the murders. Who told you this?"

"You should know that a reporter does not reveal his sources. I would go to jail before I did that." Seth's eyes sparkled behind his thick spectacles. Sarah assumed he was quoting a line from an old film; he was thoroughly enjoying the drama of the moment. She paid for his coffee as a gesture of appreciation for the act and left him there.

Information could not be contained very well these days, Sarah reflected, as she drove home. Too many people had too much access to a variety of media channels for most things to stay quiet for long. If more than one person knew something, it was only a matter of time before people could Google it, see it on YouTube, read about it on a blog, or have it appear in any of thousands of news sites all around the globe. Oh, and eventually show up in the old media, newspapers and television.

CHAPTER 25

February 15–16

Sarah tried not to bring her projects home, but something was working in the back of her mind, and she found herself at the old iMac in her home office after dinner. It had been her night as chef; she had prepared a lovely salmon glazed with teriyaki sauce and orange juice along with a simple salad. She and Dev had a clear agreement that whoever cooked did not have to clean up, so she had some time. She had gotten more curious about the apparent gap in Roberta's résumé and decided to Google her. Her last name was somewhat unusual—Brightchild—which ought to make her easy to find. And, indeed, she was everywhere—two or three pages' worth of press releases, articles, the corporate website—but there was nothing from before she started to work at the insurance company. Perhaps her name had changed? Although Roberta wore no wedding ring, Sarah had assumed she was married, though she couldn't have said why. She thought there might be something interesting to learn about Roberta but didn't think she had the resources to uncover it. Perhaps John did?

Next, she checked out Arthur's obituary. She hadn't found it necessary or appropriate to attend the memorial service, though a few people in the company had; so this was the first time she had learned about his personal side. Or, rather, the side of Arthur that he didn't bring to work at Martech. Not speaking or thinking ill of the dead was not a custom Sarah subscribed to. The obit listed several civic organizations he had belonged to—not surprising for someone trying to get ahead; they were mostly of the Chamber of

Commerce variety rather than charities. He was also, she was more surprised to learn, an enthusiastic gardener and—this line caught her attention—an "investor in start-up companies." She would call John in the morning to ask if he was aware of either of these findings, and if he could find out more about them. They might not mean anything, but at this point it seemed useful to follow up on any unexpected information.

Maybe it was time to get together with Jen again. There was more that she wanted to ask her. She would try to get on her calendar this week. With that thought, Sarah turned off the computer and went to join Dev in the living room.

Sarah placed two calls when she got to work in the morning, one to John and one to Jen. Both calls went straight to voice mail. She hoped for a call back and left her mobile number for both of them—she had no important meetings today, so she would leave her phone on. Shortly afterward, John returned her call, and they agreed to meet for lunch. Paperwork took up most of the morning; she had a report to write for Mike on his project, and just before leaving for her lunch with John, she tried Jen's number again. This time, Meredith picked it up. "Jen's out at an appointment." she said crisply. "I'll tell her you called."

"When do you expect her?"

"She said not to expect her until late afternoon or possibly tomorrow morning."

As Sarah left the office building, she became aware of the tension in her body; she reached back and noticed that her neck and shoulders were especially tight. Why? She realized that she was worried by Jen's absence. It was certainly not unusual for someone to have an appointment away from the office, but at Jen's level in such a formal company, it was odd to be vague about when you would be back. Sarah's training and experience made her especially aware of situations and behaviors that were exceptions to the norm—they were usually clues to what was really going on, regardless of how people rationalized them.

John was waiting for her in the "cheap and cheerful" Chinese restaurant they had chosen. Sarah let John choose the dishes; although his family had lived in San Francisco for several generations, he could read some Chinese ("restaurant Chinese," he would say), and Sarah subscribed to the Bay area assumption that all the best dishes were written on posters on the wall in a language she couldn't read. Indeed, though the place looked like a dive, the food was splendid, and she preferred not to ask what parts of various animals were used to make it so. Some things were better for non-Chinese people not to know.

"So, what do you have for me?" John had kept his curiosity in check while they ate.

"Nothing very tangible, John, but a couple of things that struck me as interesting. I went as far as I could in researching them, but I assume you have access to other sources of information. First, I noticed that Roberta Brightchild seems to have emerged full-blown, like Botticelli's Venus on the half-shell—" (Sarah had discovered that she and John shared a passion for Italian Renaissance art "—about ten years ago. There is nothing earlier that I could find on Google or LinkedIn. She must be in her mid-forties now, so that seemed odd to me. I thought you might be able to find out if she had gotten married or divorced or somehow changed her name around that time."

"I can check the public records—and not everything is absolutely public, so there are other ways I can research it. What else?"

"This may be completely irrelevant, but I noticed in Arthur's obituary that he was a private investor in start-ups. He certainly kept that quiet; his attitude toward Staticon seemed unusually conservative and mistrustful—not what you would expect from a man who took risks on new businesses. Is there anything you can find out about his investments?"

"That's a tougher one because of SEC regulations. But I will see what I can do."

"Before you go, John, can you share a little information with me now? I know you questioned everyone on the thirty-third floor about who was where on the afternoon of Arthur's murder. Was there anyone seen there other than the people we already know about? Both Penny's and Tom's desks face outward, so one or both of them could have noticed someone entering the conference room or even walking along the passage."

"Nobody except the usual suspects—including you, of course."

When Sarah got back to her office, she found a message from Jen. Her voice sounded a little shaky. "Sarah, this is Jen. Yes, I'd like to see you. How about breakfast tomorrow morning? I'm a little... indisposed right now. Just send a text to my Blackberry to confirm a time and place." Indisposed—that could mean a lot of things, none of them good. Sarah did as Jen asked. *Meet u @ 8, Bette's.* Bette's Ocean-view Diner was in Berkeley, across the bay. Not very convenient, but Sarah knew that Jen lived near the beautifully and expensively reno-vated 4th Street shopping area there. It seemed worthwhile to do the reverse commute in the morning to be able to speak freely with Jen.

CHAPTER 26

February 17

If there was anything that made a drive to Berkeley worthwhile for a denizen of San Francisco, it was Bette's potato pancakes, complete with sour cream and applesauce. They reminded Sarah of the latkes her grandmother used to make. "You don't have to be religious to like latkes," her father often said. She was looking forward to the meal, though not necessarily to the conversation. She arrived early, as she had planned, to put her name on the list—there were no reservations, and sometimes the list was quite long. Today, however, it was remarkably quiet, and she was quickly shown to a booth in the back of the tiny restaurant. By the time she saw Jen, the place had filled up, and there was a welcome buzz. Normally, Sarah hated noisy restaurants, but today she wanted background noise to cover the conversation she expected to have with Jen—and the noise was a warm, friendly sort of cacophony.

When she first sighted Jen and waved to her, she could only see that she was wearing some sort of hat, which was unusual. By the time she reached the booth, Sarah could see that what appeared to be a hat was actually a large gauze dressing, incompletely and incongruently disguised with a beret. "What happened, Jen?" Sarah was shocked, though not as much as she might have been a few weeks before.

Jen settled in; they ordered their hot drinks. "I think I'm supposed to say that I stepped on a rake." It was a weak attempt at humor, but Jen's voice was stronger today. "In fact," she continued, "someone sideswiped my car the day before yesterday, and I spent a lot of hours

in the emergency room at Alta Bates getting my windshield extri-
cated from my scalp."

"That is just awful. I hope whoever did it had good insurance."

"Well, in fact, it was a hit-and-run situation. Luckily, I wasn't
going very fast, and my car was close to the curb. I had just
unbuckled my seatbelt, about to pull into my driveway. Then it
hit me. I was stunned—probably concussed—for a little while.
One of my neighbors heard the crash and ran out to help me; she
called the police and the ambulance and stayed with me until they
came."

They were interrupted by a waitress—server, Sarah supposed,
would be a more politically correct term, but they were definitely
waitresses. Bette's waitresses always looked as if they were going to
call you "Honey" in the classic diner fashion, even though most of
them wore a collection of studs and hoops through various parts of
their anatomy. Several, including the friendly young woman who was
standing by their booth, had apparently spent a lot of money on body
art. Sarah wondered how the sleeve tattoos might look twenty years
and thirty pounds later. *Note to self*, Sarah thought, *get to the gym this
week*. Sarah and Jen both ordered the potato pancakes with plenty of
sour cream and applesauce.

Sarah leaned back in her chair and blew on her tea, even though it
wasn't hot anymore. "Did you see the car at all?"

"I think the car had no lights on." Jen's gaze broke away and she
bit her lip. "I surely would have seen it coming otherwise. I don't
even remember hearing it, though my street is very quiet. And, of
course, afterward I saw and heard nothing for at least a minute or
two."

"Did your neighbor see or hear anything?"

"She said she heard the sound of a speeding car and then the crash.
It's very unusual for cars to speed in the neighborhood; there are a lot
of 'traffic calmers' at the corners but unfortunately not close enough
to my house, I guess."

Jen dumped two huge spoonfuls of sour cream on her latkes, and
then pushed half of it off. A waitress with mid-sized earplugs came

around with a pot of tea in one hand and coffee in the other, and Sarah held her cup out for a refill. She set it down on the table, and some tea sloshed onto the butcher paper covering the table as she caught Jen's eye. "So what do you think happened?"

Jen's voice was so low that Sarah had to lean forward to hear. "Someone tried to kill me." Sarah sat up straight and nodded once.

It seemed a bit odd to be discussing a murder plot over latkes—what would her grandmother have said? Still, the pancakes were as good as she had remembered. Jen allowed herself a half-smile. "These always make me think of my grandmother's cooking."

"Mine, too," Sarah said, slightly surprised. "Where did you grow up?"

"Just outside of Amsterdam, near the coast. Noordwijk." Sarah knew the place, having conducted meetings and training sessions at a large resort hotel there.

"I didn't know that Dutch grandmothers made potato pancakes."

"Mine did. She grew up with Jewish friends before the war and learned how to make them." Without waiting for the usual question, Jen said, "She didn't know Anne Frank, but they would have been contemporaries."

Sarah hoped there would be a time later when she and Jen could have a normal conversation about their lives; Jen was definitely girlfriend material, she thought. Alison would enjoy her, too, though she was considerably younger than either Sarah or Alison. That would have to wait—at least, until she knew for sure that Jen had nothing to do with the murders. In a hardboiled mystery story (Sarah went through periods of passionate excess in her reading genres, then tired of one and switched to another), Jen could have hired someone to sideswipe her and give her a cover story. After all, she was not hurt as badly as if it had occurred when she was traveling at a higher speed. That seemed highly unlikely, though. Who would agree to do something like that? She supposed that since there are hired killers, there are probably hired injurers, perhaps for insurance fraud. That rang a faint bell in her mind. Hadn't Roberta once worked for an insurance company?

"Do you have any idea who might want to do you harm?" Sarah asked.

"Not a clue. I'm not a person who makes enemies, generally."

"Is there a chance that you know something that could be dangerous to someone?"

"If I do, I don't know what it is." Sarah had to be satisfied with that.

CHAPTER 27

February 18

It was Thursday, a beautiful, crisp, sunny winter day. Sarah walked half a block down Mission Street before she stopped and fished through her purse for her sunglasses. They were cold where they rested against her cheeks, but she didn't mind. It was a whole lot better than winter in Minnesota, where she had gone to college. By midday, one could enjoy walking around the streets of the city without a coat. Friends from elsewhere often teased Sarah about her experience of "winter." Having lived in colder places, she was both aware of her good fortune and satisfied that she had paid her dues. Going to the snow was one thing; it was voluntary and generally had a positive purpose, such as skiing. Having it come to you uninvited was something else again.

Sarah looked forward to seeing Alison later in the day. In the meantime, she had about an hour to spend on her "mind map" and timeline and she had a lot of information to add. John had been true to his word and had found some information about Roberta. He had promised to share it with her later today, warning her that it was extremely confidential and that she might find it shocking. Sarah had no idea what to expect. Information about Arthur's investments were, he said, more difficult to come by. She knew that John had spent time with Jen earlier in the week; they could compare impressions.

Sarah was beginning to wonder whether it was time for the two of them to have a formal discussion about boundaries. Although she was acting in a semi-official capacity as the liaison with the company, she realized that she and John had never clarified what was and was not discussible. She was not exactly clear on what he could legitimately tell her, and for that matter, she was not especially certain about what was OK for her to share with him. They seemed to have formed an "odd couple" partnership that was starting to feel rather like a friendship—but with a specific purpose and strict limitations. So far, they trusted one another to stay aware of both.

They were to meet at Embarcadero 4, one of four large, unattractive buildings located near the Bay, built during the '70s. They looked as if it they been designed by a dysfunctional committee. Clearly, they had had to compromise on the most innocuous possible design. Sarah, heading for the meeting, walked past a piece of sculpture that looked like a disused building site. It was called the Vaillencourt Fountain. Homeless people gathered there at all hours; it was a sort of social center. There was certainly some value in that, she supposed. It served another purpose by making the Embarcadero buildings (all four of them) look soothing and functional by contrast.

For once, she got to the meeting place ahead of John and settled on a stone bench near some running water—someone's idea of a softening feature for the building. Not a great success, but useful for their purposes today.

John arrived, wearing a suit and carrying his briefcase. "I photocopied some news articles that might interest you," he said, after a quick greeting. Sarah held her curiosity in check while John settled next to her, reached into the case, and pulled out a file folder. The first paper he offered her was a copy of an official name change document. The name was changed to Roberta Brightchild from Rachel Benning. That name sounded slightly familiar to Sarah, but she couldn't quite place it. The document was dated June 17, 1992. John then handed Sarah a copy of an article from a Florida newspaper dated April 10, 1981. It was about a young schoolteacher who had had a sexual relationship with one of her pupils, a fourteen-year-old boy named Evan Clausson. It had caused quite a sensation at the time—Sarah remembered the case; it was unusual in that the adult involved was a woman.

The teacher claimed that the boy was very mature for his age and that they were in love with one another. She was convicted of child abuse and sentenced to twenty years. There were several similar articles from other papers. Finally, John produced a clipping with a small inside-page article mentioning that the notorious teacher had been paroled; her sentence was shortened for good behavior. The article mentioned that she had taught many inmates to read. The article was dated May 5, 1992. *There is no question*, thought Sarah, as she looked at one of the photos in an early article. Roberta Brightchild was Rachel Benning.

Sarah had picked up a chai latte on her way to the meeting; she looked down at it now, as if there might be answers written in the foam. "John, how on earth did Roberta get that first job with the insurance company with something like that on her record?"

"According to my sources, at the time, the parole and probation people there were known for helping promising parolees get a fresh start. I'm sure they assisted with the name change and helped her get a decent job—of course, in an industry that does not cater to children—and the rest was due to her hard work and ambition."

Later, over drinks at a recently opened wine bar, Sarah was catching up with Alison's love life and work hassles. "You're quiet tonight." Alison had noticed that when she stopped talking, Sarah made encouraging noises but didn't offer anything. "Are you OK?"

Sarah drained her glass and looked up at her friend. "I'm fine. I've just had the chance today to wonder if you ever really know anyone... no matter how close you think you are."

"Well, I am who I am; you know me. I have to be honest. I have such a bad memory that I couldn't remember a lie from one time to the next. If I tell the truth, I don't have to try to remember what I said. I think Mark Twain said that first, but I agree."

Sarah smiled. Living a lie—or taking on a completely new identity—would be stressful. One would always be looking over one's shoulder in case someone from the old life might show up and recognize him or her. It would be impossible to ever feel safe.

CHAPTER 28

February 19

Secrets. Everyone seems to have them, thought Sarah. All of the self-confident, powerful people on the thirty-third floor had them, along with everyone else. Sarah remembered a time when she had visited the Danish Parliament building—the Folketing—with a friend whom she had met when she was an exchange student. Her friend, Ingrid, was now a government minister. Ingrid took Sarah to the gallery and looked down on the members going about their activities. She pointed out a tall blond man and then a slim businesslike woman. "They're lovers. And those two over there—they're divorced, because she had an affair with the man who is speaking now. Oh, and these two men have been in a relationship for years."

Sarah was astonished. "How do you know all this? I certainly couldn't do that for you in the House of Representatives in D.C.; the tabloid newspapers hire people to dig up that kind of information."

"It's a small country," Ingrid said with a smile. "Everyone knows everyone's business here."

She had rather thought that was true of Martech, especially for someone like herself, to whom people confided things. While she certainly had Too Much Information about some of her clients, she had been deeply shocked by what John had shown her yesterday. What other secrets existed behind those smooth public faces? It was late Friday afternoon, and Sarah was staring at her mind map. She added some cryptic notes next to Roberta's name—she wouldn't take any chances of the information escaping. If Roberta had nothing to do with Ed and Arthur's deaths, she had paid her dues, and Sarah would just have to try to forget what she knew.

How about the others who seemed to have either the opportunity or a motive, what secrets did they have? She already knew about Jen, that she and Ed had been lovers years ago. Tom? Well, she supposed that Tom was gay—but in San Francisco, that hardly qualified as something to keep secret. Penny...there was something there, Sarah was nearly certain. She was almost too perfect on the surface and very self-controlled. It would be difficult to learn anything Penny didn't want you to know. Bengt might be just who he appeared to be: a brilliant entrepreneur with a hefty ego, a sense of humor, and unusually good social skills. But maybe he had a dark past as a drug smuggler? Sarah smiled as she thought about a Swedish-American mafia; having spent time in Scandinavia herself, she knew that there was a dark side (Steig Larssen's novels were among her favorites), but Swedes tended to be one-faced, WYSIWYG (What You See Is What You Get). The Nordic countries would not have produced a Machiavelli.

Maybe she would find a reason to have a chat with Penny next week. There was a problem with that, though; as an internal consultant, Sarah had a lot of freedom in the way she responded to clients' needs and requests but very little ability to initiate anything. Maybe Dev would have some ideas for her—he was a good "shadow consultant," her behind-the-scenes advisor. His background was enough like that of her clients that he could give her a similar perspective.

Sarah pulled into her driveway. She and Dev lived in what they liked to refer to as "Pacific Depths." Others called it Lower Pacific Heights (at least real estate agents did; it was formerly the Upper Fillmore, but as prices escalated in the '90s, the name of the neighborhood went upscale as well). Just off California and Divisadero, their home was small and unpretentious, but comfortable. They had just about been able to afford it in the late '80s when they bought it. They certainly wouldn't be able to afford it now, even with prices somewhat depressed in the past couple of years. They were meeting friends for dinner tonight, but there was an hour or so to chat.

Dev was happy to be consulted. His current project was unexciting, though financially rewarding, and he took a lot of pleasure in helping Sarah from time to time. He had to admit that her work was often a lot more interesting than his. He had never felt competitive with her; they had quite different interests and skill-sets, and he was proud of her accomplishments. He did like it, though, when she asked his advice. And when, on occasion, she took it.

"Dev, you're a lot more cynical than I am about what goes on behind the scenes in big corporations," Sarah began, after she had changed for their dinner party.

"You've noticed that I don't work for one anymore," he deadpanned.

"OK, but it pays half our bills," she reminded him, slightly defensively. A late Baby Boomer, Sarah still felt a little uncomfortable working for "the man," as her older siblings would have said. "Anyhow, I need to understand more about what goes on between the ears of people who are not quite at the top but want to be. There's always a lot of talk about teamwork, but whenever I work with an executive team, I'm aware of undercurrents. Sometimes I can bring them out in the open, but more often I just discount for them in order to arrive at what's really going on. I assume there are a lot of private agendas that won't get discussed and try to get them to set those aside and find some common ground."

Dev scrunched up his face as if she had brought up some painful memories. "I know exactly what you mean," he said. "I can remember any number of meetings where I knew perfectly well that everything anybody said was designed to make someone else look bad rather than to try to solve whatever problem we were dealing with. After one too many of those, the life of a free agent began to look very attractive. Less security, but also a lot less aggravation, and I can sleep at night."

Sarah was envious of the latter—especially recently. "So if you could read between the lines of what people said, what were they really thinking? What was motivating them?"

Dev smiled. "It pretty well boiled down to competition. Competition for the boss's approval, for a specific job, or for scarce resources.

Sometimes it got pretty underhanded, but the 'perp' always had an innocent explanation for why he had revealed a colleague's mistake or failure or indicated the vast stupidity of his or her idea."

"Something I've noticed," Sarah added, "is that when somebody is made to look bad in one meeting, he or she nearly always finds a way to return the favor in a subsequent one...but it all sounds reasonable if you weren't at the previous one."

"It can get pretty intense," agreed Dev. "I think the last straw for me was when I saw two VPs get into a physical fight in the parking lot over what one of them had brought up to the CEO about the other. It wasn't pretty; both of them were out of shape, red in the face, and using language I hadn't heard since high school. That did it for me."

"I remember. You needed a pretty stiff drink when you got home, and then you disappeared into your laptop for several hours."

"Yes...researching how to start and run a consulting practice."

"So, blood combat is not that unusual in the executive suite."

"Well, figuratively, anyhow. Your people seem to have taken it much farther."

Sarah leaned back on the sofa, crossed her legs, and closed her eyes for a moment. Dev's comment brought her back to the question she had been pondering earlier in the day. She sat forward. "Any ideas about what I can do to find out more about the underlying motivations? I'm not really in a position to ask them directly; my role doesn't lend itself very well to initiating such a conversation."

"It seems to me," Dev said thoughtfully, "that there is a larger issue here. You were asked to help manage the changes involved with the merger, right?"

"Of course. By Ed, months ago. But I'm not sure who my client is now. Arthur certainly wouldn't have asked for my help, and he hasn't been officially replaced as yet. I suppose I could check in with Roberta again." Sarah wasn't planning to tell Dev what she had learned about Roberta.

"Oh, and one more thing before we go." Dev glanced at his watch. "I always found the admins to be a fount of information if you treat them well. But I'm sure you knew that already. And it's a holiday weekend, have you forgotten?"

Sarah had. She was often embarrassed when she forgot birthdays, anniversaries, and holidays like Valentine's Day, which would be tomorrow. Dev found that amusing, usually. Unlike many of his male friends, he always remembered special days, and now he handed Sarah a box of the exquisite artisan chocolates from Recchiuti Confections in the Ferry Building. Sarah was not sure whether to eat them or place them under glass as a work of art. It was going to be a very pleasant weekend.

CHAPTER 29

February 22

"Penny, I appreciate your taking the time to talk with me. As I mentioned on the phone, I am trying to update my notes on the merger process so that I'll be ready to pick up on it right away when someone is named to replace Arthur. You are really the one person who has been engaged with the process all the way through."

"I'm happy to do it, Sarah."

Penny looked around her at the décor of the new, upscale restaurant where they had gone for lunch. Coincidentally, this was the very building, an old post office, where her father had worked as a young man. He would certainly not recognize it now, she thought, nor would he recognize her in her chic business suit and fashionable haircut, eating at a restaurant like this. His greatest ambition for her, she recalled with a flash of anger, was to meet and marry a man with a steady job and the means to move to the suburbs. There was no money for tuition, of course. She would have liked to study science, perhaps become a teacher. Instead, she had worked her way through Heald Business College and started on a series of administrative jobs. Penny had put up with several bad bosses in her career. Sexual harassment of varying degrees, she learned, was to be expected; she had found ways to handle it tactfully. Supervisors who micromanaged her were more difficult. She always managed to stay one step ahead of them, though. No matter how many extra hours she had to put in, Penny made sure that her work was impeccable. When she was hired at Martech, Penny saw an opportunity. Most of the other admins left their desks at the official closing time, but Penny was often at the office until eight or nine o'clock in the evening. She asked for additional responsibilities. Before long, she began to be noticed by more senior managers, who also stayed late. Within a year, she had become a personal assistant to a VP; and a year after that, Ed had asked her to work for him. That was three years ago. And what a three years it had been. She wrenched her attention back to Sarah, who had been speaking for the last minute or two.

"…and did you want to share an appetizer? They are quite wonderful here."

Penny was relieved that she hadn't missed anything important. She didn't see Sarah as anyone who could help her career, but you never know. No reason to be rude to her.

"Fine, Sarah. You choose." They ordered nonalcoholic mojitos, refreshing on this sunny day that hinted at spring; some tapas as appetizers to share; and two of the salmon dishes for which the restaurant was famous. Sarah knew it would take a while to arrive, given the size of the lunchtime crowd at this popular place. There would be plenty of time to learn more about what Penny knew and was willing to talk about.

"So, as I recall, you started working for Ed about three years ago?" Sarah began. Ed had not been her client at the time, but she remembered noticing Penny when visiting with others whose offices were near Ed's. She had appreciated Penny's professionalism, though her authoritative formality seemed a little odd in a person so young.

"Yes, that's right." Sarah could see that she would have to work hard for any useful information. She began to regret that she had not suggested a real cocktail—though Penny would probably have refused it. "What was his focus at that time? I don't recall."

"He was always responsible for mergers and acquisitions, but Martech was mostly doing small ones at that point."

"So when did Staticon enter the picture? I didn't hear about it until about six months ago."

"That has been in the works for about a year."

A slight sneer crossed Penny's face. It gave away her pleasure at being able to "one-up" Sarah with insider knowledge. People like Sarah, educated women, always seemed to look down their noses at Penny. Sarah had it all: an easy job—just talking with people, after all—and, from what Penny heard, a good-looking husband and a grown daughter, who was a lawyer. Marriage had not been a priority for Penny, at least so far. The men she knew were not marriage material. She would be fine with an older man, perhaps divorced or widowed—not interested in children (Penny imagined that children would be too much of a distraction from keeping the right husband happy), but well off. For a while, she was quite sure that Ed would be that person. A wave of regret and resentment passed by, and her cheeks felt warm; she hoped Sarah would not notice. Of course, Sarah did notice—but as she didn't have a ready explanation, she filed her impression away for later examination.

"How was it going, from your point of view? I believe you sat in on a lot of the meetings. I know how much Ed trusted and respected you. I suppose he talked with you about it."

Penny patted her hair and went on, flattered by Sarah's attentive attitude. "Yes, Ed took me into his confidence. He was quite happy with the progress at first; Staticon was just what we had been looking for."

Sarah made a mental note of the "we." "Because..." Sarah encouraged.

"Oh, because they had innovative products and a list of clients that didn't overlap much with ours." This was not news to Sarah, but she listened respectfully. "And then, about two months ago, things changed."

"How so?"

"We learned that there were some problems we would be acquiring along with the company." *So far, nothing new*, thought Sarah. How much more would Penny say? "They had hidden a very big legal problem. Something about a patent. I didn't understand the details, but it worried Ed. He decided that the Staticon people he was working with were not trustworthy. We might be able to deal with the legal issues, but not if we had to defend people who were senior employees."

Sarah noticed that Penny was wearing a pair of small pearl stud earrings, almost exactly like the ones Roberta often wore, though of course not of the same quality or value. She guessed that Penny had given her as much information as she could or would; so over the remnants of a very good lunch, she tried to change the subject. "You and Ed worked very closely together, I can see. You must miss him."

Penny's face, unguarded for a moment, showed Sarah by the tightened jaw muscles and flushed cheeks that she had hit a nerve. "It was strictly a professional relationship. I don't get involved emotionally with the people I work with. It was sad, of course, but he wasn't a friend or anything."

"What does your future look like now?" Sarah decided to pursue this topic over coffee and tea.

"I don't anticipate any problems." Penny had recovered her poise. "I know several people who would like me to work for them. And they certainly can't sort out the merger mess very well without my help."

"Do you have any idea who might replace Arthur?"

"Well, it won't be Jen, I know that. I hear that Roberta has engaged a search service and is looking outside. In the meantime, she has asked me to keep on top of things and report to her temporarily."

How does she know that it won't be Jen? Sarah could still be surprised at how much information the executive assistants were privy to.

The bill was hefty, and Sarah didn't think she could use her corporate credit card, so she used her personal card. Dev would raise an eyebrow but wouldn't complain; he had suggested this, after all.

After returning to her office, Sarah wondered what she had gained. A confirmation of her understanding of the merger issues, yes. But there was something else as well: the few moments when Penny had dropped her guard suggested that there had been more to the relationship between Penny and Ed than she wanted Sarah to know.

CHAPTER 30

February 23

It was time to take stock. At a certain point in a consulting engagement, Sarah always gathered her notes—anything relevant on her laptop, desktop, or smartphone, as well as the variety of sticky notes that tended to collect on various surfaces. In this case, she also had the mind map and timeline she had been working on. She would summarize the key issues and questions. Usually, once this had been done, she would come to a clear understanding of the group's issues and would then be able to design an intervention to help them to deal with the key ones.

Rather than spread everything out on her desk, she made sure that everything important was on her laptop, and then tucked the papers into her briefcase. Just to be on the safe side, she deleted all the notes on her desktop. This was work to do at home, she decided. Working at home was a new concept for Martech, even though the rest of the corporate world had taken it up years before. She called her manager, Sylvia, the head of HR, to say that she was coming down with a cold (this was true, actually) and would be working from home for the rest of the day.

Later, as she laid everything out on her dining room table, she could see that there had been some progress in understanding—or at least making some educated guesses—about the issues that were related to Ed's death. She put off thinking about Arthur for a while, even though she knew that his death and the attempt on Jen's life were part of the larger system. Still, she felt that the key to it all was in someone's original motivation to get rid of Ed. The notes she finally posted around Ed's name read:

- *Jen was losing ground to Arthur in terms of influence and opportunity. She and Ed had been lovers in the past, is that relevant?*
- *Arthur wanted Ed's job.*
- *Bengt was about to be tossed overboard and possibly blamed for the patent issue.*
- *Roberta had a major secret that Ed might have known about; he wanted her job and might have planned to "out" her in order to move up.*
- *Penny had some sort of relationship with Ed beyond being his assistant* (Sarah was certain of that after her lunch meeting). *Was she being rejected for someone else?*

Sarah hesitated before adding a note with a question.

- *Why would anyone want to blame Jen for the murder?*

And branching below that she added:

- *Arthur, to get rid of a rival?*
- *Penny? Any jealousy there if she knew of Jen's previous relationship with Ed?*

She couldn't see any advantage to Bengt or Roberta in pinning the murder on Jen. Sarah then began thinking about Arthur. She posted his name and below it she put these notes:

- *Jen, in a fit of rage after she was attacked in a meeting in front of her team.*
- *Jen's team members in order to protect their beloved boss.* That didn't sound very likely, Sarah thought.
- *Bengt, in order to restore the deal he had made with Ed.*
- *Roberta?* Sarah couldn't think of a motive, unless she had killed Ed and Arthur knew it.
- *Penny?* Well, anyone who worked for Arthur might be tempted to annihilate him, but Penny seemed too cool a character to do so; she would just move on and up. Unless, of course, Arthur had something on her.

And finally, she posted a note with Jen's name. Below it she put:

- *Penny, if she was jealous—but this took place after Ed was gone, so not much reason to do it.*
- *Roberta, if Jen knew and threatened to reveal her secret.*
- *Jen, herself, to throw people off her trail.*

That was lame, Sarah knew. Not a lot there to work with. And she hoped she had not been too quick to decide that Jen was an unlikely murderer; she tried to keep her personal feelings at a distance when she thought about any client engagement, and she was approaching this in a similar way. She would see John again tomorrow; maybe something new would have emerged. Then again, the trail might be getting a little cold. Sarah sneezed, making an honest woman of herself, and made herself a hot lemon drink.

CHAPTER 31

February 24

Sarah stepped into her cubicle and stopped, horrified. She stared, open-mouthed, at the devastation. Her cubicle had been trashed to within an inch of its plastic life. Drawers were pulled out; the trash can was emptied on the floor; her locked cupboard was hanging open, looking like a floozy with an open dressing gown. She felt angry and violated. The contents of all of her confidential files were strewn around on the floor or the desk. She gathered up everything she could see and began checking to see what was missing. Sarah was not a neat freak at home, but in the small cubicle she called her office, there was really no room for disorganization. She knew where everything was kept, and she updated her files regularly.

She had a good idea of what would be missing, and she was right. The files on the merger project were gone, along with everything else she had worked on with Ed. Whatever sense had told her to delete files on her computer yesterday before leaving had been both right and timely. Sarah did not think of herself as a religious or even a particularly spiritual person (she was never clear on the difference, though many of her friends seemed to be), but she did trust and follow her intuition. And her intuition had not misled her this time. Fortunately, between her regular consulting and coaching engagements and her current avocation as a corporate detective, she had not had the time to update her paper files; every note she had made was on her laptop, which was safely in her briefcase (she glanced up to make sure it was still where she had set it down), or at home, where she had left the mind map and timeline.

This was getting a little too personal, Sarah mused, as she began to clear up the mess. Obviously, somebody knew that she was helping John, or at least exploring the situation. Was she meant to take this as a warning? She called John and, without explaining why, asked that they schedule their meeting a little later in the day and a little farther from the office.

When they met later, she told him what had happened. John was briefly sympathetic but quickly got back to business. "The message seems to be consistent with the other things you've learned recently."

"Yes, maybe it's *too* consistent. I've been wondering about that." Sarah was thinking out loud. "It's almost overkill. Oops, bad metaphor. Maybe I am supposed to believe that this is all about the merger when it really has nothing to do with it."

"Why do you say that?"

"It's just a hunch." Sarah looked out the window of the café for a moment and then back at John. "When I'm working with a client group, and there seems to be an obvious cause for problems they're having, I've found it useful to be skeptical. The most visible explanation, the one that seems logical, isn't always the real reason things happen the way they do. And there have been times when someone wants to convince me that X is the cause of the problems (usually a person or another group in the organization), when it is really Y or Z or both, or all of the above. I just have a sense of that going on right now." Sarah also explained to John why she wanted to meet in this rather out-of-the-way café. "Clearly, someone knows that I am working with you; I'd just as soon meet less frequently or at least be more careful about the venue."

At home that night, Dev was clearly upset by the news of the office trashing. His usual good-natured humor deserted him, and he frowned. "I'll make it a point to be at home all day for the next few days," he said, "in case whoever did it decides to check your home office."

"I don't think that will happen, Dev. I'm pretty sure that whoever did it was not really looking for anything—just wanting to scare me and maybe influence my thinking about the case."

"All the same, I think this is getting a bit dangerous. Maybe it's time to take a break. We're long overdue for a winter vacation." Dev picked up a handful of brochures, all of which sported palm trees, from the coffee table.

"I just spent our winter vacation money on a dress for Astrid's wedding. She was not going to have me one-upped by Molly Moneybags."

"You mean Jason's mother."

"Molly Marburg. Sorry, I couldn't resist." Sarah was not especially looking forward to the round of bridal showers and other wedding-related events, especially those that involved the female side of Jason's family. He was really a fine young man, and Sarah was happy to have him in their lives, but she was glad that nearly all of his relatives lived on the other coast; her few encounters with them so far had been awkward, formal, and brittle.

"Well, I didn't spend all of it, really, but I do feel as if I need to see this through," she went on. "My sense is that we are close to a solution. I hope you can put up with my Nancy Drew act for just a little while longer." Dev chuckled. He knew that Sarah was only half-joking. When they met, she had told him that her heroines were Eleanor Roosevelt, Marie Curie, and Nancy Drew. Though Nancy was fictional, the three shared some characteristics with one another and with Sarah: curiosity, boldness, and independence. Not to mention the aggravating tendency to do things their own way, regardless of other people's wishes. Dev did not like to think of himself as Ned Nickerson, Nancy Drew's inept boyfriend, whom she frequently had to rescue. Nonetheless, he was beginning to feel a little marginal in Sarah's life, as her work was more intense than ever. Dev was not, under ordinary circumstances, a jealous man. He had never worried about the men that Sarah worked closely with; he trusted her commitment to him. It was the job itself that seemed like a rival these days.

CHAPTER 32

February 25

It was time for a casual conversation with Roberta. Perhaps she had a plan to replace Arthur and move further along with the merger. Sarah wanted to make sure that she stayed on top of this; she had committed to Bengt that she would let him know if there was a reason for him to stay involved, and she felt that she could do it without compromising her philosophy. It seemed appropriate for her to check in and see if Roberta wanted or needed her to move forward with the plans she and Ed had originally made to try blending the leadership team.

She called Tom, who answered in his usual crisp, precise, cheerful tone, "How about late this afternoon, Sarah? I see that Roberta has a cancellation around four; will that work for you?" It did.

On the way up in the elevator, Sarah cleared her mind as much as she could of the information she had gained about Roberta. This would be, to the degree possible, a strictly work-related meeting. Tom greeted her warmly, apologized that Roberta was not yet back from a previous appointment, ushered her into the office, and magically procured a cup of tea and a tray of tea biscuits. He was a real treasure, Sarah thought. "How was Roberta so lucky as to find you?" she asked.

"Oh, I appeared on her doorstep in a basket one day. She was good enough to take me in." Tom had a very charming dimple, Roberta noticed. She hoped he had a nice boyfriend at home. Roberta appeared a minute later, wearing a beautifully cut suit in a jewel-tone green that set off her white hair. Seeing this made Sarah think for a moment that she should stop covering the gray that had lately sprung up in her own nondescript brown tresses.

"I just thought I'd check in, let you know how things are going with John, and see where you are with the merger, Roberta. I wondered whether we should move ahead with the originally planned meetings, or if it's better to wait until you have a replacement for Arthur."

Roberta settled gracefully into a chair opposite Sarah. She rarely sat behind her desk for meetings. "Thanks, Sarah. You have anticipated me. I've decided to take this on myself for now. I'd certainly like your help and was about to call you. Can we set up a meeting with Bengt and his team for next week?"

"Well, let's talk a bit first about what you'd like to accomplish. What are your longer- and shorter-term goals for the process at this point?"

"I'd like to keep it simple. One company with two different pathways to achieve remarkable results. Let's set a goal for the meeting of getting a clear commitment from Bengt and his team to stay on, and then we can agree on next steps to create Staticon as a separate division."

Sarah left with the distinct impression that Roberta was relieved about something. Corporate life was moving forward. It all seemed a bit too smooth; Sarah felt uneasy. As she left, she noticed that Tom was not at his desk. This was extremely unusual; to Sarah's observation, he almost hovered around Roberta in a protective way. Presumably, he did have an independent life, but one would not know it from his behavior at work. She waved as she passed him, walking back to his post on Roberta's "doorstep."

Alison provided little comic relief after work. Her relationship was in one of its difficult phases; her plumbing and technology needs had been minimal of late, and she was getting tired of her boyfriend's failure to disentangle from the demands of his ex-wife. Sarah was in no mood to empathize, as she was still rather frazzled from the events of the week. They parted earlier than usual.

CHAPTER 33

February 26

John and Sarah seemed to be meeting more often these days. Obviously, it was becoming more important for him to show some results from his investigation, but Sarah suspected that these meetings were also an intellectually stimulating break for him. She did not flatter herself that there was anything more to it than that. She was in good shape for her age but had gotten used to the invisibility of being a middle-aged woman around younger men. And, of course, she didn't care. Well…not much, anyway. Today they were back at the more distant coffee shop, and John suggested they review the players who had had the opportunity to kill Ed or Arthur. All of them were single (with the exception of Arthur) and had no substantiated alibi for the time of Ed's death, which occurred somewhere between 1:00 and 4:00 a.m. John wanted to discuss their possible motivations.

"Jen—unlikely, I think, but could be either ambition or anger. As for Penny, I am sure she had a relationship with Ed that was more than professional, though I have no direct evidence of that other than her facial expressions and flushing. She might have killed him out of anger or jealousy. Perhaps if she knew about Jen's previous relationship with him, she might have tried to point your attention toward her. Arthur certainly had an interest in Ed's job and maybe something beyond that. If we knew more about his investments, we might understand more. As for Bengt, I don't think there would be any advantage to him in killing Ed, as he and Ed had an agreement. On the other hand, I can see why he might want to get rid of Arthur, who was opposed to that agreement and in a position to change it. So if Arthur killed Ed, then Bengt might have done Arthur in, I suppose, but it seems far-fetched. Roberta...well, we know that Ed wanted her job, and perhaps he knew her secret. That would provide a strong motivation for her to get rid of him, and I think Jen would have seemed a convenient scapegoat to her as well."

Sarah ended her summary with a shrug of her shoulders. "Tom could have done it, I suppose, but I can't imagine why he would take a chance like that. He has a good situation, and I don't see how either man could have threatened his well-being or security." Sarah felt that she had come to a dead end. She was beginning to tire of the whole situation. At the same time, she would not like to have it come to her attention in a bad way again, especially if she could have done something to head it off. She often felt like this when she had a really frustrating engagement with a client group—and that, she reflected, was often just before a breakthrough in her thinking about how to approach the situation and get some positive movement going. Perhaps Dev was right about taking a break.

"Oh, and I have been meaning to ask you something, John," she said as she rose to collect her coat and bag. "Where was Ed's phone when he was found? I am still puzzled by his call to me—and I wonder, why did that not fix the time of death as after three?"

"I should have mentioned that. It was in his back pocket. We didn't use that time because, as there were no clear fingerprints on it, we could not assume that he was the one who made the call."

"So, I have been thinking about this the wrong way around all along." Sarah was reporting on her day to Dev. They were wrapped up in sweaters and scarves and sitting in front of the fire. Their in-floor heating system had chosen the coldest day of the winter to go down, and it would be tomorrow at the earliest before it could be fixed. The damp chill was getting to Sarah. Oliver, looking grumpy, was clamped to her lap almost in desperation as the only warm place he could find.

"I think you were right the other day, Dev. I do need a break. From the weather, from this case, from my clients. Let's go to Florida."

"Why Florida? Except for all the obvious reasons, of course. You haven't liked it much in the past, as I recall." Sarah came clean with Dev. "Of course I do want a break and some time away from work and with you. Some sun and sand would be great. But I also want to check out a hunch that has been lurking in the back of my mind this afternoon, and Florida is the place to do it. Sylvia should be OK with it; I am overdue for a vacation, and I am between major projects."

"I'm on it." Dev pulled out his laptop and began to scan the travel sites. "Is tomorrow afternoon too soon?"

CHAPTER 34

March 4

Miami seemed much the same as it had the last time, which meant that its charms would be exhausted for Sarah after a visit to Vizcaya and a day at the beach. They were staying in Coral Gables, an attractive neighborhood with lots of shops and restaurants. It was rather reminiscent, in fact, of many neighborhoods in San Francisco, only more pastel. Sarah had promised Dev that she would relax and enjoy the weather and the slow pace for three days, and he had agreed to her plan for an excursion on the Wednesday of their week in Florida.

The three days passed quickly. Sarah and Dev both enjoyed the leisurely pace and the brilliant weather. Sarah had to attend conferences in Florida on a regular basis, but they were always held in the low season, when the heat and humidity reduced the hotel prices considerably. Her attitude toward Florida was improving as they strolled along the streets, hit the beaches, and dined in some exceptional restaurants. They luxuriated in the long evening conversations and lazy mornings that had once been a more frequent aspect of their relationship. They made a commitment to do something like this twice a year from now on.

On Wednesday morning, they picked up their rental car near the hotel and set off for LaBelle, a small town at the edge of the Everglades. It was about a three-hour drive; the air was balmy and sweet, and they were soon sorry that they had turned down the option of a convertible. They pulled into the town, drove along the main street, and found a coffee shop called Mary's Place with an open parking spot right in front of it. Mary's Place looked like a setting from a '60s sit-com, with its neon signs, mini-jukeboxes, and leatherette seats in the booths. Dev settled down in one of them with a copy of the Miami Herald and waited for Mary, or whoever her successor was, to bring him some coffee. The shop was nearly empty except for two elderly men sitting on stools, nursing their coffee and talking about the local high school football team, from what he could hear. Sarah left Dev there and set off for the courthouse. LaBelle was the county seat of Hendry County, and the courthouse was just a few blocks away; they had passed it as they drove into town.

About an hour later, Sarah was back. "You look satisfied with yourself," Dev said as she slid into the booth across from him.

"It has been a productive hour," Sarah replied. "I'll tell you about it after lunch."

They ordered the lunch special from a comfortably-built woman who looked exactly as if she had stepped out of the sit-com. She wore a gray uniform with a white apron; it was freshly washed but bore faint evidence of previous soup stains. She wiped her hands on a towel as she approached them, smiling. "You're not from around here, are you? Heading for the Everglades?" It was a slow day, and the waitress—Maureen was her name—was chatty. She had a niece who had moved to San Francisco a year or two ago. She might go and visit her there one day; she had always wanted to see the Golden Gate Bridge and the Hollywood movie studios. Sarah and Dev did not enlighten her on the distance between her favored attractions.

"Haven't I read something about your town?" asked Sarah. "The name sounds so familiar to me. But I think whatever it was happened quite a while ago."

"Nothing much happens here," Maureen said cheerfully. "Oh, except we did have a scandal some years back—did that make the news in San Francisco?" She seemed flattered.

"Oh, yes, wasn't it something about a schoolteacher?" Sarah acted eager to hear the local gossip.

"Oh, you do remember it, then. Yes, she was a pretty thing, too. We could never understand why she went after that boy. Half the men in town would have gone with her if she had crooked her little finger."

"Did you know her?" Sarah brushed some imaginary crumbs off the table. She did not look at Maureen.

"Not her, but I knew the boy's family. Neighbors of ours."

"Whatever happened to the boy, do you know?"

"He was a bright boy. Went off to the University. His parents both died in a car accident while he was away. Never did see him again after their funeral. I heard he went west somewhere, maybe to Texas."

"Did the teacher ever come back?"

"Oh, no, she couldn't show her face here. Funny, I had nearly forgotten about all that until just the other day when I came across some old photos. Evan—that was the boy's name—he used to play with my girls. They liked to dress up and give plays, and the photo was one I took of them being pirates. I was going to give that picture to my older daughter; they were good friends. I might have it here."

She ducked behind the counter and returned with a faded Polaroid print. Click! Sarah felt things coming together as she stared at the photo.

"I do wonder whatever became of Evan. Such a nice boy he was, and such a terrible thing to go through. She was a bad one." The waitress shook her head sadly, dramatically, as if she had been directly involved in the story.

On the drive back to Miami, Sarah told Dev what she had learned in the courthouse and what the photograph had revealed. She nearly sent John a text but decided to wait until she saw him to explain what she had found. She opened the window on her side and let the wind blow the last of the cobwebs from her brain.

CHAPTER 35

March 8

Any stress relief provided by a week away was neutralized by the number of e-mails and phone messages waiting for Sarah on Monday morning. Mostly, they were the usual requests for her services, reminders of meetings (including Roberta's meeting on the merger set for tomorrow afternoon), and copies of follow-up documents that got sent to anyone who might have a reason to complain if they were left out of the loop. Sarah would have been happy if she were left out of any number of loops; as she operated across the company, she ended up getting information she neither needed nor understood, and which was only peripherally related to work she was involved in. Still, it all had to be dealt with somehow, if only to put it in the "FIFI" (file it and forget it) folder she had long ago established.

The one message she felt a need to respond to right away was from Bengt. The message read, "Haven't heard from you, can we have a pre-meeting meeting?" Sarah felt a little guilty; she should have been in touch before leaving, if only to say something neutral but upbeat about the meeting. He would have gotten the message. She sent him a quick text to say that she had some time in the early afternoon if he would like to do a walk-and-talk. Sarah had set herself the goal of getting rid of her vacation weight gain before it had a chance to settle in; the mother-of-the-bride dress had just barely fit, with no room for expansion.

Bengt was waiting for her in the lobby, as tall and blond as ever. She would get a decent workout trying to keep pace with him. They decided to walk along the Embarcadero as far as AT&T Park and back. Sarah had never gotten used to corporations getting naming rights to sports stadiums; it just sounded silly to her—as if the corporation was fielding a team of out-of-shape executives.

Bengt got right to the point. "I wanted to check in with you before the meeting. I hadn't heard anything and assumed that was good news, but I was a little surprised when Roberta called this meeting. I thought that things would be delayed until someone was appointed to replace Arthur. I don't know whether to be worried about it or not, but I do want to make a decision soon. At this point, my team and I don't have any assurance that we can really build something here; I never did have that talk with Arthur about a package that would make it attractive for us to leave. My dad used to say that you can't keep one foot on the boat and one foot on the dock for very long."

Sarah stopped a moment to catch her breath. "Bengt...I think you should wait until tomorrow to make any decisions; if the meeting goes the way you would like it to, you can just move forward—but I assume that you have developed a BATNA." She hurried to catch up with him.

"A what?" Bengt slowed his pace a little and looked at Sarah as if he were trying to read her lips.

"I guess you haven't been through my negotiation course," Sarah puffed. "That's a term invented by Roger Fisher and William Ury to describe a way to prepare for a negotiation. I think that's a good way to prepare for this meeting as well. It means Best Alternative to a Negotiated Agreement. It's a way you know you can get your needs met if you can't make a good deal with the person or group you're negotiating with. Any deal you make should be better than your BATNA."

"I do have options, Sarah. I have one or two good offers, but it would mean starting over with a different technology or going into a different business entirely. Not ideal."

They had completed their circuit just in time. Clouds were gathering, and the sky looked ominous. "Let's see what happens tomorrow, Bengt. I'm not hearing anything negative." That was as much as she could safely say. Bengt nodded slowly and thanked Sarah as they parted ways on the elevator.

Sarah spent the rest of the afternoon developing an agenda for Roberta's meeting. It was simple and straightforward and, she hoped, would finally lead to some resolution of the merger issues. It had been many weeks since she had started this project with Ed. That thought reminded her that the phone call, the one that had started her down this path of playing detective, had probably been made by Ed's killer, not by Ed. Sarah shivered.

As she packed up to go home; her laptop bag felt oddly light. Had she left it in her cubicle when she went out walking and talking with Bengt? Could she have been so careless? She had been. The laptop containing all of her notes was gone.

CHAPTER 36

March 9

It was hard to say which was worse, the weather or Sarah's mood. One of the Bay Area's intermittent drenching late-winter storms was laying waste to hillsides; houses teetered on cliffs, and electrical power outages affected traffic lights and snarled the commute. It often happened like this. Just when it seemed as if spring might be coming, with the narcissus and redbud starting to bring back color to the world, the skies opened, and people had to sigh and tell themselves that it was making up for the drought—and at least they would enjoy late-spring skiing this year.

As she crept along toward home through the rain-clogged traffic, Sarah tried to persuade herself to be philosophical. Her backup system was at home, so she hadn't actually lost any data, especially as she hadn't used the laptop while on vacation or since she got back. Still, whoever had it now would probably not have much trouble getting access to her files. Sarah had carelessly used her date of birth as a password. She was suddenly seized with a need to call Dev and ask him to reprogram their home security system, which used the same password.

Sarah was not known for her memory of details, and she was more concerned that she would forget a password or security code than that someone else might figure it out. She used the speed dial (remembering to put her earpiece in first) and was relieved to find Dev at home. As she spoke, she could hear that her voice was shaky—whether with rage or fear, she couldn't have said right then. Dev heard it too and

immediately suggested that they meet at a favorite neighborhood restaurant, a place where they could get some comfort food and relax. He
promised to reprogram the security system before he left the house.

Olivier, the young French owner/chef, greeted Sarah warmly and
seated her at a corner table facing the door. Dev arrived shortly afterward, his hair damp and curly from the rain. He kissed Sarah and
settled into the chair opposite her. "You forgot your umbrella again,"
Sarah reprimanded him with a wan smile.

The Curbside Café was an intimate place with an eclectic menu—
everything from pot roast to curry. Tonight was a pot roast night for
Sarah; she needed all the comfort she could get. Over a carafe of the
house red, she let Dev talk her down from the frazzled state she had
arrived in. The warm Parisian bistro ambience, pleasant but unas-
suming wine, and delicious food did their job. By the time they left
for home, she had stopped blaming herself for the loss of her laptop
and had even begun to think about replacing it with the latest and
lightest version.

Sarah went to bed early; it had been an exhausting day. She needed
to be in good shape for the meeting tomorrow. It would be challenging enough, even without her other concerns. Still, sleep didn't come
easily that night, and when it did, she had the elevator dream again.
This time, she stayed with it long enough to see the door begin to
open, but before she had a chance to step out, her alarm went off.

CHAPTER 37

March 10

The rain had stopped, and it took Sarah less time than she had expected to get to work. As she walked into her cubicle, she did a double-take. There was her laptop, sitting neatly on her desk. Could it have been there all along? She didn't think so. She opened it and turned it on. Instead of the photo of herself and Dev in Portofino, which was her usual screensaver, there was a photo of a shipwreck with an oil slick. Somebody's idea of a macabre joke, maybe— or another message to her to stop messing around in this business. She sent a quick text to John, whom she was to meet after Roberta's meeting today, letting him know what had happened. He sent her a return message, asking her to be careful. It suddenly occurred to her that laptops could be booby-trapped, and she quickly shut it down.

Sarah's plan for the meeting was simple. She would ask Roberta to kick it off by stating her goals, and then she would ask the others to add anything else they hoped to achieve in the meeting. She would post the agenda on the wall of the conference room and then do her usual facilitating, which, in the case of most meetings of senior executives, meant finding tactful ways to get them to let others have some air time (especially the lower-ranking participants who were usually the ones who had the information required to make important decisions). She might call for a decision when she thought they were ready, or bring them gently back if they strayed from the topic. If extraneous issues popped up, she would put them on a "parking lot," a large sheet of paper posted next to the agenda for items to follow up at later meetings. If there were strong disagreements, she might work with those in opposition until they could find a compromise or alternative they could both live with. Once they had checked off all of the items on the agenda, she would ask them to summarize and list action steps and deliverables, who was responsible to do them, and when they would be due. It was not very different from other meetings; this kind of plan generally worked well for Sarah and her clients.

The conference room was cold when Sarah arrived at 9:30 a.m., a half hour before the meeting was scheduled. She shivered as she entered. It was not so much from the temperature; it was more from the memory of the last time she had been in the room and saw Arthur under the center table. In order to suppress that thought, Sarah began rearranging the room. What looked like a large conference table was really made up of four smaller ones. She formed three of them into a U-shape, so the room looked less formal and everyone had more space. The fourth table would hold the coffee, tea, pastries, and fruit that the catering service would soon bring in. She set up a large flip chart stand and pad facing the "U." It all looked very normal to Sarah, and she sat down near the stand to relax, just as the catering crew entered the room.

The meeting participants began to arrive. Jen arrived with Henry; Bengt arrived with his team, including Carla, Vijay, and Craig. Penny walked in briskly. Her jaw was tight; Sarah assumed that she wasn't entirely comfortable. Her role was rather undefined at this point, but she had a great deal of relevant information. Everyone was chatting nervously over cups of coffee. Roberta made her appearance on the exact stroke of ten. Tom followed her in, sat down at the end of the table, and opened his laptop. Sarah assumed he was there to take notes.

Roberta was wearing a simple, elegant, black silk dress; a Hermes scarf; and a persimmon-colored jacket slung over her shoulders. She always managed to look powerful, businesslike, and sexy at the same time, Sarah thought enviously. "Thanks for being here," she said. "I think this meeting will be a short one. I have some news to give you."

CHAPTER 38

March 10

"John, I was stunned. As was everyone else. " Sarah shook her head. "The last thing I expected was for Roberta to announce her resignation. And then she simply turned around and walked out, followed by Tom."

"Did she give a reason?" John would never understand people walking away from a good job. Nobody in his family would do such a thing, and he knew that his older relatives would be very skeptical when the time came for him to leave the force and open up a law practice.

"None. It was short and sweet. I rather think she will be gone tomorrow."

"Do you have a clue about what might be going on, and why she might want to leave—or is it that someone else wanted her to leave?"

Sarah had already been planning to fill John in on what she had learned in Florida, but it seemed even more important to do so now. "I don't know whether or not this has anything to do with her decision, but I discovered something that might be relevant. Tom was Rachel Benning's schoolboy lover. And I think he still is."

John was silent for much longer than was usual for him, then said, "I thought he might be gay. It never occurred to me that he might be...maybe you would say 'in a relationship' with his boss."

Sarah nodded. "They were both very private. I guess they had to be. He must have found her again, or vice versa, after she was out of prison and on parole. They would have had to be exceptionally discreet then. I suppose that has continued."

"This puts a new light on the motivations we discussed the other day, doesn't it?" John was thoughtful for a moment. "I think we need to know where she—or they—are headed for."

He made a quick call and apparently got no response. "Sarah, do you have a way of finding out if they are still in the building?"

Sarah called Jen's mobile number. She had almost given up when Jen answered. "I'll just run up to the thirty-third floor and walk down that way while we talk," said Jen, in response to Sarah's request. Sarah heard a whoosh, then Jen's stilettos clicking on the marble floor in front of the elevator; then silence, so she must have stepped onto the carpet. "Hi, Penny," Sarah heard her say, then more silence. Then, "Penny, have you seen Tom? He doesn't seem to be at his desk." More faintly, Sarah heard, "I saw him walk to the elevator about a half hour ago. He was carrying his briefcase, so I assumed he was going to another meeting. Maybe the same one Roberta had left for a little while earlier. I suppose she has a number of people to talk to."

Sarah put her phone in speaker mode, so that both she and John could hear the call. John whispered, "Finish the call; we need to go."

"Thanks, I need to run," said Sarah, leaving a slightly puzzled Jen at the other end of the line. She stared at John. "What do you mean, we?"

John put a tip on the table, slung his jacket over his shoulder and grabbed his briefcase. "I don't have my car, it's in the shop—I walked over here. You drove, right? We're going to the airport."

"John, should I really be part of this?"

"You have a car, and you know what Roberta was wearing, there's no time to wait to do this the kosher way. Don't worry; I'll take care of any speeding tickets."

On a normal early afternoon, SFO (San Francisco's international airport) was about thirty minutes from downtown. John and Sarah made it in twenty. They parked in front of the International Terminal, leaving Sarah's car to the mercy of the parking police.

As they hurried into the terminal, John directed Sarah, "Buy a ticket at the shortest line so you can get through security." There were flights leaving in the next couple of hours for London, Zurich, and Hong Kong.

"Without luggage, I'm likely to be seen as a terrorist." Sarah thought she knew what John had in mind; she hesitated for a few seconds, then turned toward the check-in line for the flight to London.

"With a bag that size, you don't need to worry," John said. Sarah looked down at her major indulgence, a large Coach beige leather satchel that served today as both a briefcase and a purse. An eBay find, not full price, but the real thing. Big.

She felt reckless as she pulled out her credit card and bought a round-trip, business-class seat on the London flight. (*In your dreams, Sarah*, she said to herself.) She took the ticket and ran with John to the Priority security line. He showed some ID that enabled him to get through without showing a ticket, though he did have to pass through the newly installed whole-body imaging *machine*, as did Sarah. She preferred it to the invasive pat-down that always followed a trip through the old machines—her youthful athletic activities had meant an early knee replacement, and it always set off the machines, causing her to be rewarded with an extra inspection.

At the other end of the security gauntlet, John grabbed her hand and sped toward the gates, but Sarah said, "Wait! We don't know where they're heading. I've a hunch that Roberta will be flying first-class. Let's try the First Class Lounge; it's on the right, between gates."

Sarah had been in it once when she accompanied a senior executive client to an international meeting. It was smaller than the other airport lounges, quiet and discreet. They practically flew down the walkway. As they entered the lounge, the concierge at the desk looked alarmed; she was not used to red-faced, disheveled people, who certainly did not look as if they were flying first class, disturbing the atmosphere. John flashed his ID, and they continued into the room, standing where nobody could get past them. Sarah scanned the comfortably appointed room full of executives tapping away on their iPads or laptops. The persimmon-colored jacket did not make for a good disguise. Roberta and Tom looked up, made the obvious calculation, and sat back resignedly.

CHAPTER 39

March 11

A young man was sitting with his back against the Martech building, peering out under his cap, his hair hanging in his face. Sarah, arriving early, assumed he was one of the homeless people who sometimes hung out in the area, providing a contrast with the sleek buildings and well-dressed businesspeople. She imagined that he was keeping an eye out for the building guard, who normally made sure nobody was loitering near the entrance. Suddenly, he leaped up and approached her. She stepped back, startled, and Seth, more disheveled than usual, nearly careened into her.

"You misled me! The murders had nothing to do with the merger at all."

"Seth." Sarah spoke slowly in words of one syllable, as if she were speaking to a three-year-old. "You. Made. That. Up. I did not say they did."

"I thought I had a real story. It was something the major media were ignoring." Sarah couldn't help feeling a little sorry for him. She had a soft spot for anyone who was really passionate about his or her work. He did have a lot to learn, but then, he had a lot of time to learn it.

"Come on in. I'll buy you a coffee. But do something with your hair first." He shook it out and tucked most of it under his cap. "I'll give you fifteen minutes of my time. I haven't even dared to look at my e-mail this morning. I will be heads down for the rest of the day.

I'm sure people learned about Roberta and Tom from the news last night, and I will be inundated."

Seth made an effort to sound professional. "Yes, my colleagues did some good reporting on the evening news. But maybe I can get another angle on it. How did your experience as an internal OD consultant help you to solve the case?"

Sarah repressed a laugh. "I didn't solve it, Seth. I took my role as liaison to the police seriously, but Inspector John Chu put it all together. I did spend some time thinking about it as if it were a consulting engagement."

"Meaning...?" Seth was definitely improving in his ability to ask questions rather than confront his subjects with accusations.

"Meaning that I listened a lot, asked questions, and assumed that there were layers of meaning and associations that were unspoken. I did not take anything at face value." Sarah stopped for breath. "Then I looked for patterns and connections, and if I discovered anything that seemed just a little bit odd or unexpected, I followed up on it. And I trusted my hunches, while staying open to the possibility that I was completely wrong."

"That sounds like what a good investigative journalist would do."

"Good observation, Seth." Sarah grinned, tossed a tip on the table, and strode off to begin what would undoubtedly be a very busy day.

CHAPTER 40

March 18

John, Alison, Sarah, and Dev were enjoying the evening. It was almost the spring solstice and unusually warm for March. Sarah was dressed up in a Bay Area sort of way, which meant that she was wearing a long black skirt over her comfortable shoes and a sort of "art to wear" fitted silk jacket, which she had paid too much for at a recent fine crafts fair. Alison, of course, set the bar high in a stunning jewel-tone green ankle-length dress that set off her vigorously red hair. The men were dressed nicely but inconspicuously in what might be called "business casual for the evening."

Sarah usually avoided anything resembling matchmaking, but she had grown quite fond of John, knew he was single, and thought he and Alison might enjoy one another—Alison was perfectly comfortable dating somewhat younger men. She had finally dispatched her previous boyfriend, having grown tired of his preference for dealing with plumbing problems rather than communicating with her.

The four of them were seated on the candlelit terrace of a restaurant in the Presidio with a view of the San Francisco Bay. The miniature chandeliers that served Alison as earrings tonight swayed in the breeze and sparkled in the flickering light.

"Your wife missed her calling," John was saying to Dev. "She is seriously good at detecting."

"That is what she does for a living...not quite the kind that you do, but she has to go beyond the obvious to find out what's really going on in her client organizations. And maybe it's time for you both to fill us in on what really happened after you found the two of them."

Sarah had been putting off telling the story, saving it for this evening; a little more than a week after Roberta/Rachel and Tom/ Evan had been arrested. The past few days had been taken up with preparations for Astrid's wedding, which would be happening in two weeks. Sarah's sleep had been deep and seemingly dreamless. There were no elevators, but if there had been, the doors would probably have opened on a Felliniesque scene involving caterers, florists, and musicians.

John began, "I called for backup, and we arrested them. They both seemed resigned and didn't put up any resistance. Sarah had told me what she learned in Florida, and something just clicked. They had been heading for Zurich—to be closer to their money, I suppose. Roberta had been salting it away in a Swiss bank, perhaps knowing that one day they might have to disappear."

"I doubt that she could have predicted why, though," interjected Sarah. "Of course, Ed knew that Roberta was not happy with him and that he might not survive the completion of the merger. Besides, he wanted her job, and somehow he learned her secret. Tom saw to it that he didn't live to tell it. I imagine they thought they were safe, but they hadn't counted on quiet little Penny. She knew all of Ed's important secrets. Pillow talk, I suppose…and she ingratiated herself with Arthur to save her job by telling him what she knew. Arthur, inept tactician that he was, let something slip to his former assistant, forgetting that the 'AJT'—Admin Jungle Telegram—would mean that the word got back to Tom the same day. Apparently, and this I've learned since last week, he only said something like, 'Roberta had better treat me well, because I have some information about her that she wouldn't want broadcast.' That was enough to set off Tom's alarm, though. He walked into the conference room after the meeting was over and coolly dispatched Arthur."

"So Tom was also responsible for the attack on Jen and the goings-on in your cubicle?" asked Alison.

"Yes; apparently those were meant primarily as distractions and to scare people off. And the whole issue of the merger, which seemed so central to everything, had nothing to do with it at all. Now that Jen is temporarily—eventually permanently, we hope—in Roberta's role, things should go ahead as planned."

"I have just one more question," said Dev. "Why the call to Sarah at 3:00 a.m.?"

"The phone was in Ed's back pocket," John said, then smiled. "Apparently when he was pushed into the cabinet, it was pressed down enough to make the call he had programmed for the next morning, which was a call to Sarah. So it was—to be polite—a back-pocket call."

With that, they all raised their glasses to the sunset, toasting old and new friendships and a hope for a more peaceful second quarter.

ACKNOWLEDGEMENTS

During the past year as I have been learning that writing fiction is much harder than writing anything else – and also much more fun – I have been blessed with the support of many friends, teachers, and mentors.

Thanks to the friends who took the time and trouble to read and critique early versions: Diana Harrison, Dena House, Jan Schmuckler, Bev Scott, Deak Wooten, Russ and Pat Silverstein. You made me focus and showed me what was missing, while encouraging my efforts.

I learned so much from the Mystery Writers' Conference at Book Passage and was inspired by speakers such as Jacqueline Winspear and Hallie Ephron. Feedback from Tony Broadbent, Rhys Bowen, and Elizabeth Kracht was timely and valuable.

I am very grateful for the feedback from pre-publication readers: Lynn Andia, Elaine Biech, Charles Evans, Dena House, Bev Kaye, Dena House, Pat Newmann, Judith Olney, Veronique Rostas, Charlene Rothkopf, and Kris Schaeffer. You gave me the thumbs-up I needed to move ahead.

My writers' group continues to give me the time and space to ask for critique; to listen and learn. My reading group pushes me to read authors who surprise and delight me and teach me about writing.

The wonderful people I have consulted with, coached, and taught over the past 40 years or so have contributed to this book in countless ways. I didn't kill any of them off and if any of them read it, they may find aspects of themselves among Sarah's favorite clients.

Most of all, I am grateful to my daughter and fiction mentor, Heather Davis. She shared her knowledge, was both unsparing and generous in her feedback, and gave me the loving encouragement I needed both to get started and to finish the project.

ABOUT THE AUTHOR

B. Kim Barnes is the CEO of Barnes & Conti Associates, Inc., of Berkeley, California, an independent learning and organization development firm. She has had over 30 years of experience in the fields of management, leadership, and organization development, working globally with organizations in many industries. A frequent speaker at professional conferences and meetings, Kim has published many articles in professional journals and books and is the primary developer or co-developer of popular Barnes & Conti programs such as *Exercising Influence, Constructive Negotiation, The Mastery of Change, Inspirational Leadership, Intelligent Risk-Taking, Applied Creativity, Leading Global and Virtual Teams, Managing Innovation,* and *Consulting on the Inside.*

The second edition of her book, *Exercising Influence: A Guide for Making Things Happen at Work, at Home, and in Your Community,* was published by Pfeiffer/John Wiley in 2006. Her most recent business book, co-authored with Beverly Scott, is *Consulting on the Inside: A Practical Guide for Internal Consultants,* published in 2011 by ASTD Press. After completing this book,

Kim was inspired to begin writing a tongue-in-cheek corporate mystery series with an internal organizational consultant, Sarah Hawthorne, as the protagonist. The first book of the series, *Murder on the 33rd Floor,* was published in early 2012. Kim has long thought that successful internal consultants have a similar skill set to the great fictional detectives. Frequent long-distance air travel has provided the time for her to test that assumption through writing what she calls "Nancy Drew stories for adults."

Kim resides in the San Francisco Bay Area with her husband and two cats.

For more information about Barnes & Conti's programs, visit www.barnesconti.com

For more information about the Corporate Mystery series, visit www.corporate-mystery.com

Made in the USA
Charleston, SC
11 March 2012